Shabash!

Shabash!

by

Ann Walsh

BEACH HOLME PUBLISHING LIMITED
Victoria, B.C.

First Canadian Edition

This edition published by
Beach Holme Publishers
4252 Commerce Circle, Victoria, B.C. V8Z 4M2
with thanks to The Canada Council
and the B.C. Ministry of Small Business,
Tourism and Culture for their generous assistance.

Editor: Guy Chadsey
Production Editor: Antonia Banyard
Cover Art and Design: Barbara Munzar

Canadian Cataloguing in Publication Data
Walsh, Ann, 1942-
Shabash!

ISBN 0-88878-355-8

I. Title.
PS8595.A585S52 1994 jC813'.54 C94-910684-4
PZ7.W3491Sh 1994

For so many reasons
this book is for
my father.

Acknowledgements

Many members of the Sikh community of Williams Lake offered me help and encouragement with this book and it could not have been written without their guidance and support. I learned a great deal from them, from how to make roti to how to put on a turban, although I am not terribly successful at either endeavour. Nor would the hockey scenes have been possible without much help from teachers, coaches and my nephew Anthony Varesi, all of whom answered my questions patiently and offered advice. Guy Chadsey at Beach Holme Publishers believed strongly enough in my story to accept it in its initial stage and guide me through the revision and editing process and Antonia Banyard took my panicky calls and made sure the missing pages were found. I would also like to thank the Ministry of Small Business, Tourism and Culture for their financial support. Thank you to everyone. I hope the finished book lives up to the faith and trust you placed in me.

1

They didn't know what to say to me at the minor hockey registration booth in the mall. It was Friday night, and the line-up of kids and parents waiting to sign up stretched past the fronts of three stores. I waited half an hour before I got to the head of the line where two ladies were taking registration.

"Yes?" said one of them. She was very fat and didn't even look up as she spoke, just kept on shuffling papers.

"I want to join minor hockey."

"That's what we're here for. What division?"

"Division?" What was she talking about? I don't know much about hockey in general and even less about minor hockey, but I'd learned how to skate last year and I thought that playing on a hockey team would be fun.

"I don't know," I said. "I'm eleven, but I've never played hockey before."

She looked up at me and stared. "Oh!" she said, her mouth falling open so far I could see the wad of gum she had tucked away in there. Then she nudged the lady beside her until she looked up from her paperwork and both of them sat there staring at me.

"I can skate though," I said, wondering why they were staring like that. There must be other kids as old as me who have never played minor hockey, even though lots of them start when they're much younger.

The two ladies didn't answer, just stared some more.

"And I've got the money right here," I said, trying to hurry things up. I could tell that people behind me were getting restless, waiting for me to finish so they could have their turn to sign up.

"Um...." said the fat lady.

"I know how much it costs. I saw it in the paper," I began fishing in my jacket pocket for my money.

"Um, I...." the first lady said again.

"But...." said the other one.

"Hurry it up, can't you?" said someone behind me in the line. "We don't have all night. Get on with it."

The two ladies looked at each other, then back at me. "Do you think we should?" said the big one.

"I guess so," said the other one, shrugging her shoulders. "Give him the forms, Sharon. I'll go and phone a coach."

"Do you really think we should?" asked the Sharon lady, again.

"Sure. Just don't take his money until I get hold of Coach Bryson." Then she turned to me and smiled. "Sorry for the hold-up," she said. "We have to check a few things out with the coach." She got up and rushed off, looking worried.

Mrs. Sharon pushed some papers across the table. "Take these and go over there and fill them out," she said. "Then come back."

I was annoyed at the thought of having to spend all that time in the line-up again. It seemed to me that the other kids had filled out their forms right at the table. Well, maybe they had picked them up earlier and had already done all that paper work, so all they had to do was pay their money. I'd never done this before, so I didn't know what the routine was.

I went over to the Orange Oasis and got a small malt. Then I sat down on a bench and went to work.

The date was printed right on the forms, September 1980, so I didn't have to worry about getting that right. The rest was easy. Name and grade level. Address and telephone number. The usual stuff they ask you for and then some questions I couldn't answer, all about position played, division level last year and other hockey stuff. I hoped it didn't matter too much that I couldn't fill in all the blanks.

By the time I finished the forms and waited my turn in the line-up again, there was a man standing behind the two ladies at the registration booth. He was just as enormous as the lady. His big gut hung over his belt and stretched the buttons on his work shirt. It seemed to me that he kept shooting quick little glances my way. When I reached the head of the line again, I wasn't too surprised when he put a flabby arm around Mrs. Sharon's shoulder and said, "Let me handle this, dear."

So they were Mr. and Mrs. Something—probably Mr. and Mrs. Fat, I thought—and he *had* been looking at me while I waited in the line-up for the second time.

The skinny lady had come back to the registration table and she sounded upset. "But Bill, Coach Bryson said to...."

"Never mind about Bryson," Bill told her. "It's a good thing I dropped by to see how Sharon was doing with the registrations. I'll handle this."

"I've filled out all the forms," I said, "and here's my money." I pulled out the wad of bills from my jacket pocket. One hundred dollars. It was a lot of money, but I'd managed to save it from my paper route and my allowance. I even had enough extra for new skates. My parents weren't going to be too pleased when they heard that I'd joined minor hockey, and there was no way they would hand over money to pay for it.

I guess the money did look pretty grubby. It hadn't been in the bank, just in my drawer where it got sort of squished and crumpled. I tried to straighten out the bills as I put them on the table, but no one picked them up. Big Bill stared at the hundred dollars as if someone had barfed all over it and the two ladies stared, too, almost as if they'd never seen money before. It wasn't dirty, just messed up and they wouldn't get their hands dirty if they touched it. I began to have a sneaking suspicion that no one wanted my money.

"We can't take...we don't allow...you aren't allowed to...." Bill's voice started out loud and angry, but trailed off as if he didn't know what to say. His wife took over.

"I'm really sorry, ah...Ron," she said, looking down at the forms to see what my name was. "I'm sorry, but we can't take your money."

"Why not?" I asked, although I was beginning to figure out what was going on.

"Because we won't have...not in this league...can't possibly...." Big Bill was trying to talk again, but he didn't get too far this time either. Once more his wife had to take over.

"I'm sorry, Ron, but we don't allow...." She didn't really know what to say either, but the other lady broke in.

"Sharon! Bill! He hasn't filled in the parental consent form. His parents haven't signed."

"Of course." Bill was finally able to talk to me. "You see, ah, Ron, we have to get your parents to sign this form so the hockey league isn't responsible if you get hurt or something while you're playing. You can't join a team unless your parents sign this." He pulled a piece of paper from the stack I had given him and dropped it on the table in front of me. Somehow I had missed it when I filled out the other pages.

"Okay." I picked up the consent form and all the others I'd completed and shoved the money back into my pocket. "Okay, fine." I turned to go.

I guess the other lady, the thin one, was feeling a bit sorry for me because she called out, "Have your parents sign that, Ron, and you can mail your registration to us and pay your fee later. The address is on the back."

"Sure," I mumbled and began to walk away. "Sure." The suspicion I'd had earlier was even stronger now. It wasn't just a matter of having my parents sign that form. I wasn't wanted in the minor hockey league. The other parents and kids waiting in line stared as I walked past them. No one was talking now, just standing there staring at me. It seemed awfully quiet for Friday night at the mall, so quiet that I had no trouble hearing Big Bill when he spoke.

"There's no way a stinking Hindu is going to play hockey in *this* league," he said.

2

I'm not a "stinking Hindu." I'm not even Hindu, I'm Sikh. They are both religions, but they're different. What Bill said was like calling someone who's Jewish a "stinking Catholic." It makes me mad.

Sure, my parents are from India, but I speak Punjabi, not Hindi. It's not the word, "Hindu," but the way people say it; the way Bill spat it out as if it were a swear word. And I don't stink, and even if I *were* Hindu, I wouldn't stink, but people like him will never get close enough to either Sikhs or Hindus to find that out.

Last year my Grade Five teacher did a unit in Social Studies. She called it "Getting to Know Us," and everyone in the class had to research someone else. Find out all about them; where they were born, where their parents came from, what church they went to and all of that stuff—and then give a report about that person to the rest of the class. When we did the reports I found out that kids in my class went to lots of different churches and that some of their parents and grandparents came from other countries, too.

Places like Germany and China and England and Australia. So what's the big deal about me going to the Sikh temple on Sundays and my parents being from India?

My Grade Five teacher also taught us a new word, one I hadn't known before. Prejudice. It means that people don't like other people. Not for any good reason like they're mean or kill people or hit their kids, but just because they are different.

I'd never heard the word "prejudice" before Grade Five, but I already knew what it meant. I had lived with it all my life. Dad says it's the same in many small towns in British Columbia, towns where a lot of Sikhs live, and that we get used to living with it. I knew what he meant. You pretend you don't hear the teasing words, you try to laugh, you choke down anger. You let it roll over you and think that you really don't care any more, that it doesn't bother you, that words can't hurt you. Then something happens that hurts, really hurts.

I was hurting as I walked home after trying to register for minor hockey. *What was the big deal?* I wondered again. Hundreds, thousands of kids play minor hockey right across Canada. There must be other East Indian kids who play and Chinese kids and Native Indians and lots of others who have different religions and come from other countries. But I guess there had never been an East Indian player in my town's hockey league. They hadn't known what to say to me at the registration booth, but they hadn't wanted me to join, that was clear.

To heck with them. My parents are always telling me that I have a stubborn streak just like my grandfather, and I could feel it coming out. I'd worked hard for the money to join hockey, I was entitled to join and I was going to join!

I'd phone the coach if I got any more static. He had said that it was okay for me to send the forms in, okay for me to play hockey in the league. Now the only problem would be getting my parents to agree.

I walked quickly, angry, thinking how everyone had stared at me as if I were some sort of freak. I'm not. I am Canadian, as Canadian as any other kid in town. More so than some. I was born right here, in Dinway's hospital, eleven years ago in 1969. I've lived here all my life and my English is good. I don't have an accent when I speak English, although my Mom says that my Punjabi isn't great, that I speak it with a funny accent. I'm not very good with Punjabi spelling either; the alphabet is hard to learn. But my English spelling is better than most of the kids in my class. I've always gotten As in spelling and language and all of that stuff.

Okay, my skin is dark. I look "different." I'm the darkest one in my family, outside of my grandfather who's still in India. I've never met him, but I've seen pictures. Mom says I look like him. It's funny how the colour can be so different, even in the same family. My little sister, Baljinder, was really light-skinned when she was born. She's kept that light skin, too, the way she's kept the nickname my father gave her the moment he first saw her. We call her "Babli" and now it seems more her real name than Baljinder. It's shorter to say and suits her. She talks. All the time. Babbles even, so Babli fits her.

I know I'm really dark. Even though they call me Ron at school and not Rana—which is my real name—there's no mistaking me for a white kid. I hadn't thought it mattered much. Until now.

When we did that research in Grade Five and I learned about prejudice, I had thought that it wasn't too bad in Dinway. At least it wasn't too bad at school. There are three East Indian kids in my class this year and we get on all right with the other kids. No one calls us names or refuses to play on the same team as us in gym. The other guys, the whites, leave us pretty much alone at lunch and recess, but we stick together in our own group and don't bother about them, either. There doesn't seem to be much prejudice in our school, but I guess I'd just had my first lesson on how much prejudice the adults carry around with them.

Maybe it's because of the mill. Dinway is a small town and its major industry is lumber. That's what it says in the tourist guide book that the town makes up every year. We have one big mill in town and a lot of people drive the logging trucks or work in the bush, cutting down the trees so they can be brought into the mill. Almost everyone in Dinway works in the logging industry, and those big trucks loaded with logs roll into town all day long. Dad is a foreman at the mill. He's the only East Indian to have such an important job, but there are a lot of others from the Sikh community who work there too.

It's because of the mill, the mill and the jobs, that there are so many East Indians in Dinway. A lot of young men come over from India, looking for work in British Columbia because there is work for them, work they can easily learn to do. And Dad says that when an East Indian gets a job, he works hard to keep it.

Harder than the *gorays*, the whites. Dad says he can always count on his Sikh workers to take the shifts no one else wants and to help out if he needs someone to work overtime.

He says our people don't slack off on the job, or try to take extra-long lunch hours and coffee breaks the way some of the other workers do. Many of the men who work here have families back home in India, wives and children that they want to bring to Canada. And the only way they can afford to do that is to hang onto a job and save every penny. So the East Indian men work hard at their jobs and sometimes even share a house with other East Indian workers, putting up with shabby furniture and rooms that need painting, just so they can save more of their salary.

Dad says that things are getting harder, now. The mill had to lay off some workers and when some white guys lost their jobs and some East Indian men didn't, it got pretty tense. But things are tough all over British Columbia right now, Dad says. It's the recession, whatever that means. He's always talking about it and hoping it will end soon.

A few years ago there were lots of jobs and everyone who wanted to work was able to. Now, though, mills in some towns have even closed down and people are out of work everywhere. I guess that sort of feeds the prejudice, makes it grow. When a white worker loses his job, he blames the East Indian who kept his. And when he sits home unemployed, I guess he can think some pretty ugly thoughts, even though it's the recession's fault.

Anyway, Dinway was going to have an East Indian player—me—on its minor hockey league, like it or not. Somehow I'd have to convince my parents to sign that form.

As I opened the front door, the warm smells of cooking rushed past me; hot oil and chili peppers and fresh ginger and garlic. "Hi, Mom," I called. "Something smells good."

In the kitchen, my mother, her arms streaked with flour, was working with the roti dough. Rotis are sort of a bread-pancake that we eat with almost every meal. We don't use much bread, except in sandwiches for lunches, so Mom makes roti almost every day.

"You're late, Rana." Mom didn't look up, but kept patting the balls of dough between her palms until they flattened into perfect circles.

"Yes. Sorry." At home we mostly speak Punjabi, but Babli and I use English once in a while. Mom's own English is terrible, but she likes to hear Babli and me speak it. When Babli started school, Mom enrolled in a special class to help people learn to speak English, but she didn't learn much. She kept right on speaking nothing but Punjabi at home and to her friends and never practised her English. After a while she quit going to the classes. But my dad is really fluent. His English is almost as good as mine, which I guess is one of the reasons that he got to be a foreman at the mill.

I watched my mother as she slid the flattened rounds of dough into the hot frying pan, flipping them over after they browned. Then she put them on a rack over one of the stove elements, glowing red hot, and the rotis puffed up like beach balls. When she takes them off the rack, she butters one side lightly and stacks them and they settle down so they're pancake shaped instead of beach ball shaped. Reaching out, I took a roti from the stack of fresh ones.

"Rana! Wait! Dinner is nearly ready."

"Ah, Mom..." I grinned at her and bit into the warm roti anyway. "It smells so good I can't wait."

She smiled back, pleased. "Flattery, Rana, flattery. Go and call your father and sister, please."

Dinner was roti and dal, which I guess looks a bit like chili, but is made with beans or lentils and no meat. It also has more spices in it than chili and although they're both spiced to be hot, they taste really different. I like chili on a hot dog, but for dinner I prefer dal.

I waited until everyone was nearly finished eating before I took a deep breath and brought up the subject of minor hockey.

"Mom, Dad..." I said, tearing off a chunk of roti to scoop up the last of the dal in my bowl. "I...uh...I want to join the minor hockey league."

There was silence around the table and everyone stared at me. Then my father said, "No Rana, absolutely not."

"You didn't even take time to think about it," I said. "Just listen for a minute. I've got the money, saved it from my paper route and my allowance. I've got enough for new skates, too. And I'm a pretty good skater. Remember last winter when our school had an outdoor rink? We all had to skate in gym classes and I had to learn. I got those old skates and used to go down to the lake and practice on Saturdays."

"He's a good skater," said Babli. "Not like me. I still fall down a lot."

"So skate on the lake. Go to the arena. Why must you join a team?" asked my dad.

I didn't say anything for a while. Why did I want to join the hockey league?

"I don't know," I said finally. "Skating's all right, but I watched some of the guys play hockey at noon hours, on the school rink. It looks like fun. I'd like to try it. Just skating around by yourself is pretty lonely. I mean boring."

No one said anything for a minute or two.

"So, is it okay?" I asked. "I need you to sign this paper so I can join." I put it on the table. My mother stared at it.

"Rana, I don't think it is a good idea." My father's voice was solemn. "Hockey is a game for the whites, not for us. There will be trouble if you start pushing in where there are only white boys."

"Come on, Dad. This is 1980; things have changed. The kids at school don't mind playing on the same team as me in gym. There won't be any problems. Really."

"Things have not changed at the mill, Rana. There are problems there; problems in the lunch room where the others say our food smells and problems when...." He stopped speaking. "Never mind. We have learned to live with it, but we are adults. You are just a child and this hockey is a game for the gorays, not for us. There will be trouble, Rana. Bad trouble."

"But Dad, you're being old-fashioned. It's Canada's national sport. I'm a Canadian. I want to play hockey and...."

"No, Rana. I forbid it."

Then my mother spoke for the first time. "Palbinder," she said to my father. I sat up straighter in my chair and listened hard. I knew she was serious; she never calls my dad by his name unless she's angry or very upset about something. "Palbinder, I think it would be a good thing."

"So? But I do not," said my father. I could see he was surprised by what my mother had said.

"A good thing. Yes. Rana is a Canadian boy and it is right that he should do things that so many Canadian children do. Rana is like a young bird, stretching his wings to see if they are strong enough to take him away from his home, his nest. We must give him room to fly."

"Bird?" said Babli and giggled.

"Be quiet," said my mother.

"So we must give our son room to fly? More likely to fall," said my father.

"Then think of, not flying, but of crossing a bridge," said my mother. Babli looked as if she was about to giggle again, but I frowned at her and she didn't.

"Bridge?" asked my father. "What is all of this, Manjeet? First Rana is a bird and now he is a bridge."

"No, you are not listening to me. Rana is not a bridge; he must *cross* a bridge. Or maybe build one. It is time the Sikhs tried to mix more with the white community. We adults find it hard; we stay with our own kind, talk to only those who are the same as us. For adults it is difficult; for the children it can be easier. Let Rana join this hockey if he wishes. Let him be part of the larger community of our town."

"Larger community? Aren't you happy here, Manjeet? Do we not have a good life here, in Canada? Are not the temple and your friends and your home a large enough community for you?"

"Yes. But we are alone, all of us, all of the East Indians. We have friends, but not white friends. We are alone among the others, the gorays. This hockey, it can be like a bridge for Rana, a bridge to cross to the other world. The white world."

I stared at my mom. I had never heard her speak this way before. She stayed home, cooked, cleaned, visited with her East Indian friends. I had never thought that she felt alone; isolated from the rest of Dinway. I hadn't thought she cared, or had even noticed. Now here she was, standing up for me against my father. I couldn't believe what I was hearing.

Babli was also surprised. She's smart for a nine year old and she realized that something strange was going on. She just sat there listening, her mouth open, not even thinking of giggling. But Mom didn't seem to realize that she had astonished us.

"Think about it," she said to my father. "Rana can do more for us, for our people, by joining this hockey where there are only whites, than you or I could do in our lifetimes. If he is accepted there, then he makes it easier for all East Indians to be accepted in Dinway. I think it would be a good thing for him to begin to play this hockey game."

"We'll see," said my father. "You and I will talk about it later, Manjeet. Birds! Bridges! I think you are speaking nonsense tonight."

My mother smiled. "Not nonsense. Sense. And yes, you and I will talk about it later."

They must have talked and mother must have won, because the next morning the consent form which I had left on the kitchen table was signed—by my dad!

I mailed the forms on my way to do my papers that morning, mailed them quickly before I could change my mind. My father's words, *There will be trouble, bad trouble,* had echoed through my dreams all last night and left me feeling nervous this morning.

I was no longer sure that I wanted to join minor hockey!

3

The first hockey practice was a disaster. To begin with, it was at six in the morning and I had to persuade Babli to do my paper route for me. She hates getting out of bed early, so I had to give her two dollars to do the deliveries. If this kept up, the paper route was going to cost me more than I made!

Coach Bryson had phoned and explained that I would be playing on his team in the Pee Wee division, sponsored by the Legion. He said that we would have quite a few early morning practices because of the difficulty in arranging enough ice-time for all the teams. I wasn't too sure what "ice-time" meant, but I figured I could manage the early practices, just as long as they didn't happen too often on the three days a week the newspaper comes out. "That's okay, sir," I told the coach. "I can handle it."

I said I could handle it, but that was before I got to the practice. I'd gone out and bought new skates, expensive ones, and picked up a hockey stick at the same time. I figured I was all set to play hockey.

No way! When I walked into the dressing room, the other kids were pulling on shoulder pads, knee pads, thick hockey pants, garter belts and even some stuff I'd never seen before. I knew that the professional players wore all that kind of junk, but I didn't think the kids in the minor league had to.

There was a moment's silence when I walked in and all the guys sat there on the bench, not moving, just staring at me. I'd never met Mr. Bryson, only talked to him on the phone, but there was only one adult in the dressing room so I figured it had to be him. But he stood with the rest of the team, staring just as hard.

"Mr. Bryson?" I said, wondering why my voice sounded so thin.

He stepped out from the group and came to me. "Yes," he said. "I'm Mr. Bryson, your coach. I'm glad you could make it, Ron. Or would you prefer to be called something else? Ron isn't your...uh...your real name, is it?"

"It's okay, sir" I said. "Everyone calls me Ron at school."

"Well then, 'Ron' it is. But please don't call me 'sir.' I hate it. Makes me feel like a school teacher or a policeman. Around here, I'm just 'coach'." He smiled at me, but it wasn't a great smile; sort of tight around the edges. I smiled back anyway.

Mr. Bryson looked around the room. "Hey everyone, listen up. This is Ron, Ron Bains. Maybe some of you know him from school?" He looked around, but no one said anything. I looked around, too, but I didn't recognize any of the other players. They must all be from one of the other schools in town.

"Hi," I said.

No one said anything back.

"Ron has never played hockey before," said Coach Bryson, looking around the room again. I thought I heard someone snort, but still no one said anything. "Let's welcome him to minor hockey and make him feel at home—okay guys?"

Someone said "Hi" in a small voice, but the rest of the team went back to their lacing and strapping and tightening and didn't say anything. I found an empty spot on a bench and sat down, pulling off my Nikes and taking my skates out of my gym bag. It was awfully quiet in the room. "Big deal," I said to myself, beginning to put on my skates.

"Uh, Ron, let's have a look at your equipment. I'm a stickler for the proper equipment; cuts down on injuries and gives the players a good feeling of security."

"I could do with some of that," I thought. I wasn't feeling very secure about anything right now. But out loud I said, "All I have is my skates and a stick. I didn't know that I had to get anything else."

"Didn't I send you an equipment list? I'm sorry, Ron. Everyone else on this team has played minor hockey before, so I knew they'd have the right stuff. I guess that I forgot that you wouldn't know what you needed."

Someone giggled and a voice muttered, "Stupid raghead." The coach turned around, fast, trying to see who had spoken.

"We had a discussion earlier this morning," he said, "and I made my rules perfectly clear. Anyone who doesn't obey them is off the team. There'll be no more of that kind of language!"

"Earlier this morning?" I was puzzled. Earlier than six o'clock when the practice was scheduled to start? Then I suddenly understood. The coach had called the rest of the team together and had talked to them. He'd done it before I got there, because he'd been talking about me.

I stopped lacing up my skate. "Mr. Bryson? I think maybe it would be better if I just go home this morning. You can give me that list and I'll get the stuff for the next practice."

If things were going to be so bad that the coach had to

make rules about how the other players treated me, I wasn't going to bother with minor hockey. I'd leave, throw the equipment list away, and not bother coming back. Good thing I hadn't paid my registration fee yet. I do my own fighting when I have to, but playing hockey didn't look as if it were going to be worth the effort. Not if the ugly comments had started already and the coach had to lay down rules about me.

"I'll go home," I repeated.

"Nonsense, Ron." Coach Bryson's voice sounded funny, as if he were not sure he believed what he heard himself saying. He cleared his throat and when he spoke again his voice was stronger. "We're not doing anything terribly hard this morning, mainly skating drills to start getting everyone back into shape. You can manage without the extra equipment for today. Let's go." He turned around and shouted, "All right, everyone. Hit the ice!"

We did. But I "hit" that ice more than anyone else on the team, mostly on my rear end. I had thought I could skate pretty well, but some of those kids must have been wearing skates before they could walk. They were good! Mr. Bryson stood by the side of the rink, a notebook in his hand, watching us. We skated forwards, backwards, in circles and around and around the rink. We hunkered down into squats, lifted one leg and kicked while trying to stay steady on the other foot, jumped over pylons and even "rode" the hockey stick like a witches' broom, using it as a rudder to steer with.

Coach Bryson kept watching and writing, shouting instructions for the next exercise, occasionally calling out to someone, "Balance! Shoulder over knee, knee over foot! Both hands on the stick. Keep that stick flat on the ice, flat!"

It was only forty-five minutes, but it seemed like hours. My new skates rubbed on my ankles, the seat of my jeans was soaking wet from my attempts at the squatting drills and all the falls I had taken and my hands were so cold they seemed glued to the stick.

Finally Mr. Bryson called us off the ice, passing comments as we filed past him towards the dressing room. "You've forgotten how to stop quickly, Les. Work on it. Hey, Brian, nice cross-overs! Ken, your ankles are giving out on you. Let me check your skates before you go. They don't seem to be giving you much support."

As I went past him, he patted me on the back. "Good work, Ron," he said. "You need practice, but you've got balance and a lot of flexibility. You'll be a fine hockey player."

I couldn't believe it! It had seemed to me that I had spent most of the time picking myself up off the ice, bumbling around and making a fool of myself. I had believed I could skate well—until I watched the others showing their stuff out there on the ice.

I felt like a total wipe-out, but the coach had said "good work."

It made me feel better and I headed for the dressing room in a good mood. Sure, I wasn't the greatest skater, but I would learn. It would take a bit of time, but I could do it. I watched carefully as the others stripped off all the layers of padding, wondering if I'd ever learn how to put all that stuff on. It looked like a lot of equipment to buy and I hoped I had enough money.

"Next practice is Sunday at three. Then we'll really start working hard." Mr. Bryson was in the dressing room, checking Ken's skates. "Ron," he called to me. "I'll get you that list of equipment, but for now just make sure you have a good helmet and some gloves. The rest can come later."

Helmet? The coach and I had the thought at the same moment. I reached up a hand and touched my hair, tied up on top of my head in a white handkerchief. One of the rules of my religion is that no Sikh should cut his hair. The older boys and men wear turbans, but younger boys usually wear their hair tied up on top of their head. We call that knot of hair a "ghuta," and keep it covered with a cloth about the size of a handkerchief. It's much easier to put on than the long turban which the adult men wear; learning to wind all that material around and around your head so it stays in place is difficult and takes a lot of practice.

Would a helmet fit over my ghuta? I had no idea. I hadn't been officially baptized as a Sikh yet, so I supposed I could cut my hair if I had to. But Mom and Dad wouldn't hear of it. They hadn't had my hair cut since I was five and I knew they wouldn't approve of me cutting it now.

Coach Bryson was still looking at my head. "Les," he called suddenly.

"What?" asked Les. He was the player who'd had so much trouble stopping on the ice. He was as short as me, but he must have weighed a whole lot more.

"Lend Ron your helmet for a minute, Les. We have to see if he can get it on over that hair of his."

"But, coach!" Les looked up, his eyes wide. "But, coach, I can't do that!"

"Just for a minute, Les, not for good."

"I can't."

"Can't, Les? Or won't? Come on, pass it over."

"For him to wear? No way!"

"Les! Hand over that helmet!" Mr. Bryson's face was stern, his voice angry. Everyone else in the room had stopped what they were doing and was staring at us. "Come on, Les. Let's have the helmet."

"But my dad...I can't...." Les' voice trailed away. Mr. Bryson stood there, his hand outstretched, waiting. Finally Les reached down, picked up his helmet and reluctantly handed it to him.

"Okay Ron," said the coach. "See how it fits."

I stood and picked up my gym bag. "It's all right, Mr. Bryson. I wouldn't want Les to feel that his helmet had been contaminated."

It's a good thing that I am so dark skinned, because I was angry, very angry. If I'd had lighter skin, my face would have been bright red—a dead giveaway of how angry I was. I could feel my cheeks burning, but I knew that nothing showed on my face and my voice was calm when I spoke.

"I can buy my own equipment, thanks just the same. I don't need to try his on. Besides...."—I couldn't help it, I was furious—"Besides..." I said again, looking down at Les' huge form, "if his head is as big as the rest of him, his helmet wouldn't fit me anyway!"

Then I picked up my skates and stick and walked out. Behind me I could hear the rest of the team beginning to laugh.

Les' voice rose over the noise, whining. "Ah come on you guys, knock it off!"

They were laughing at Les, not at me. I suppose I should have felt sorry for him, but I didn't.

4

I didn't want to get my hair cut just to play hockey. Once I was baptized as a Sikh I wouldn't be allowed to cut my hair; it's one of the rules of our religion, the same way being a vegetarian is. Until I was baptized I could eat meat if I wanted to, and I could also wear my hair short if I could persuade my parents to let me cut it. But I didn't want to. Eating a chili dog at the mall or a hamburger once in a while didn't seem a big deal, but having my hair cut was different.

Something else that was worrying me was the equipment list Coach Bryson had given me. I'd looked up the prices of some of the things in the Sears catalogue and just about fallen over. I hadn't realized everything cost so much or that there was so much of it to buy: shoulder pads, elbow pads, special hockey pants—even the socks were expensive. Once I'd bought everything on that list I wouldn't have enough money left over to pay my registration fee. I counted my paper route money over and over, borrowed ten dollars from Babli, and even went to the bank and almost cleaned out my savings account. I hoped my parents wouldn't find out about that. They made me put all of the money I got for birthdays in the bank. Grandpa always sent money and I'd never spent any of it. Not yet.

I was seriously thinking about not bothering with minor hockey, just forgetting about showing up at the next practice. After all, I hadn't paid my dues yet. I had two days to make up my mind and to get all that equipment. Coach Bryson had phoned me and told me that there was a store in town that sold second-hand hockey stuff, as well as new equipment. He suggested I go there, said they were helpful and knew a lot about hockey equipment. Maybe I'd check out the prices at that store. Or maybe I'd give up the whole idea of playing hockey. That would be the easiest thing to do and probably the most sensible.

I don't know how Mom knew that I was worried about the money, but the day after my first hockey practice she called me into the kitchen. Even though my dad wasn't home and Babli was at a friend's house, Mom shut the door and when she spoke her voice was almost a whisper.

"Here, Rana," she said and handed me two fifty dollar bills. "You will need this, I think. The hockey will be expensive; there is much you must buy. I looked in the catalogue and the prices are high. Take this to help. But there is no reason for your father to know how much you and I spend. I think it will be best not to tell him." She smiled at me. I grinned back and hugged her.

Without Mom I couldn't have done it. I went to the store where they had second-hand equipment and I guess I was lucky because the only things I had to buy new were my socks and suspenders. And my helmet. The coach must have phoned the store and told them I was coming to get outfitted, because the clerks were really helpful. They had two types of helmets already picked out for me to try and one of them fit snugly over my ghuta, just squashing it down a bit. When I went to pay for everything, they gave me a ten percent discount on the new stuff, a special discount for belonging to minor hockey.

After that, I went and paid my dues. When I was finished there wasn't much left of my savings and nothing at all left of the money Mom had given me. I had a lot invested in this hockey business now, too much to even think about backing out. I'd done all right at the first practice, hadn't I? And I'd do even better at the next one.

The coach was right. Wearing all that equipment did make a difference, gave me a sense of security. Knowing I wasn't likely to get hurt by a flying puck or a badly handled hockey stick gave me more confidence—and so did the padding in the rear of the hockey pants! It was a bit harder to skate once I was wearing all the equipment, but I figured I'd get used to it quickly. Getting up off the ice was harder too, but falling didn't hurt the way it had the first practice.

All bundled up in my new equipment, with my helmet on and my new skates sharpened, I found I was trying harder and harder at each practice. Not that I suddenly became a great skater—I was still the worst on the team. I didn't have the speed that the other guys did and my ankles got tired quickly.

The coach said my balance was good and it was, but the techniques of skating, the fast stops, quick turns, skating backwards and changing directions in a hurry, were all things I had trouble with. Coach Bryson kept telling me that practice and more practice would make all the difference. So I kept on working hard at practices and Sunday afternoons I'd go to the public skating sessions at the arena and practise some more. As soon as the lake froze I'd go there to skate. It was free and there weren't so many people to watch out for when you were trying to build up speed going backwards.

I did better with the stick handling drills than I did with the skating techniques. After the coach showed me where to cut my stick down so it wouldn't be too long for my height and I got it taped in the right places, I found that controlling the puck was easier than controlling my legs. Although I'd never even held a hockey stick before I joined minor hockey, my reflexes were good and soon I could receive passes as well as anyone on the team—if I didn't fall down while I was doing it.

I learned other things, too; how to lead the intended receiver, how to pass, when to raise the puck. Those first few weeks of practice it seemed as if I learned something new every time I went out on the ice.

The others on the team were okay. There were no more "rag head" comments and no one said anything to make me angry.

Actually, no one said much of anything to me at all. On the ice we were too busy to talk. Once we got back to the dressing room everyone hurried to get changed and out of there, especially after early morning practices when we had to get to school. Someone usually said "good-bye" or "see ya" before we all rushed off, but that was about all the conversation I had with the others on the team. I didn't mind, though. Not very much.

I guess what really made me feel so different from the rest of the team was the way their parents hung around. No matter when we practised, there would be parents sitting in the bleachers; watching, cheering, shouting advice.

"Good shot, Brian!" they'd yell. "Les, check him. Check him!"

At the morning practices the parents would bring thermoses of coffee and sit in a group, huddled under the few heat lamps in the arena. Then, after practice was over, some of the fathers would rush into the dressing room, encouraging, praising, sometimes criticizing their kids and trying to hurry them up so that everyone could get to work and school on time. It didn't seem to matter that we were just practising, not playing real games; the parents were always there.

My parents didn't come to practices and I didn't think they'd come to our games, either. They didn't know anything about hockey. I guess they're afraid people would stare at them and no one would talk to them. My father didn't ask me about my hockey and I figured he was still a bit angry that I'd joined the league when he hadn't wanted me to.

I sometimes wondered what would happen if my parents showed up at the arena. I couldn't imagine my father in his turban, sitting with the other fathers, sharing coffee and talking about how the team was shaping up. I couldn't see my mother with the other women, swapping recipes or talking about where you could get a bargain on apple juice or bananas. Perhaps it's just as well that my parents stayed away.

The other parents do a lot for the hockey league. They're always having bake sales or garage sales or selling raffle tickets to raise money for extra equipment and to help with the league's other expenses. All of the players had to sell boxes of chocolate-covered almonds, to help with the fund raising. I was the first one to sell all of mine. I didn't see any point in telling anyone that I'd bought them all myself, cleaning out what was left of my savings account to do it.

We hadn't played a game against another team yet, just scrimmaged with our own players. We all rotated, playing every position, while Coach Bryson was making up his mind what spot we would play once the games began. Les had been goalie for two years. I figured he must be a good goalie because he took up so much space in the net that there wasn't much room for a puck to get past him. I'd taken my turn at all the positions. I hadn't done too badly, but hadn't been great at anything, either.

After the last practice before the games against the other teams in our division began, the coach announced our positions. There were two players for every spot, except for the goalie. Coach Bryson said that he would be doing a lot of substituting of players so that everyone got a turn on the ice during every game. But he also said he liked to have just one goalie; someone who spent every game in the net.

The line up of positions was about what I had expected from what I'd seen during practices. Brian, the tallest and strongest player we had, was centre, flanked by our next strongest players. The coach went through the team, matching names with positions. I waited for my name. It didn't come.

"Okay, guys, that's it, except for goalie. I'll let you know about that spot before the first game. Off you go, except for Ron and Les. I want to talk to the two of you."

Why did Mr. Bryson want to talk to me? Why had he asked me to stay behind after the others left? Was he going to explain that my skating was so weak that he couldn't let me play? To tell me that I didn't have a spot on the team?

I took off my skates and equipment, pulled on jeans and T-shirt and waited while everyone else, except Les, left the dressing room. I waited, afraid of what I was going to hear.

5

It didn't take the rest of the team long to clear out of the dressing room. Les and I sat on a bench, wondering why we had been asked to stay behind.

Mr. Bryson sat down between us. "Les," he said, "I want to talk to you, and I want Ron to hear what I have to say. Okay?"

"Sure, I guess." Les had his equipment bag on the bench beside him. He reached over, not looking at the coach, and began fiddling with the zipper on the bag.

"You've been our goalie for the past two years, Les. Have you enjoyed playing that position?"

"It's okay. My dad is real proud of me. He says I'm the best goalie in the league."

"But what do you think, Les? Do you like being goalie?"

"Sure. It's all right. I like it." Les was pulling the zipper on his bag up and down, making little scratchy noises. I wished he'd stop doing it.

"I don't think you're being honest with me, Les. Or

with yourself. I suspect you're scared in the net."

Les turned to look at the coach, his face suddenly white. "I'm not scared," he said. "I'm no chicken."

"It's not a matter of being chicken, Les. It's a matter of common sense. To stand there while pucks come flying at you at speeds of fifty or sixty miles an hour—it's crazy. Anyone would be scared."

Les had gone back to fiddling with the zipper, this time flicking the metal tag with his finger. He flicked two or three times before he answered Mr. Bryson.

"Sure," he said at last. "Okay, I am a bit scared. Anyone would be frightened in that net. But I can do it. I'll work real hard this season."

"I know you will, Les. You've always tried your best. But at the end of the season last year, something happened to you. Maybe you got hurt, maybe you had a couple of close calls. I don't know what it was that got to you Les, but you started pulling away from the puck. Not going into the crease when you should, missing easy shots, drawing back—"

Les interrupted him, his voice so high that it almost squeaked. "I just had some bad games, that's all. That's what my dad said."

"But we haven't had any games this season, Les, and it's happening already. You're letting too many shots past you, missing too many easy ones, holding back."

"You haven't even let me be in goal much! You've made everyone else try it out. How do you know what I'll do in a real game?" Les' voice was getting louder, shriller.

I sat there wishing I could leave and wondering why the coach was talking to Les this way in front of me.

Mr. Bryson took a deep breath. "I've let everyone else try it out because I have to find another goalie, Les. You have to get out of there before you lose your nerve completely. You need to play up front with the rest of the team for a while. I've been looking for someone to replace you in goal, that's why I've kept you out of the net so much."

Les' face went even whiter. It looked shiny and I realized that he was sweating. "I have to stay in goal," he said desperately. "My dad...."

"It's not your dad who has to go out there and face the shots, Les. It's you. And you're scared. So this year you're out of there. You don't have to stand in the net and take the shots any more. You're out of goal, at least for a while."

"But...but...." Les moved his lips as if he wanted to say something else, but couldn't get it out. He twisted his hands together and looked almost as if he were going to cry. Finally he spoke. "You won't...you won't tell my dad, will you? I mean, you won't tell him that I'm...that I'm scared of playing goal?"

"No, Les. This is between you and me. And Ron."

Les had forgotten that I was there. Now he turned to me, angry. "Now he knows, too. He'll tell everyone that I'm chicken."

"No, he won't do that, Les. I asked Ron to stay because I want him to be our goalie for this season and I wanted him to understand a bit about how difficult it can be to play that position."

I straightened up, surprised. "Me? But...."

The coach went right on talking to Les. "I wanted Ron to realize what he would face, Les. Wanted him to know that even experienced players like you can find goal a frightening position to play."

"Coach," I broke in. "Mr. Bryson, I can't do it. If Les can't handle goal—and he's played hockey for years—then I know that I can't. I'd be too scared to do anyone any good. Heck, I'm already scared out on the ice; being in the net would...."

Les looked directly at me for the first time. He leaned forward and peered around Mr. Bryson. It was almost as if he had never seen me before.

"You get scared, too?" he asked. "Of what?"

"Yes," I told him. "I've been scared since the first practice. Frightened of falling and getting really hurt, or of being knocked over 'accidentally-on-purpose' by someone who doesn't like me or of blocking a shot or even of just making a fool of myself and giving the other guys a chance to call me names. Everyone is a bit scared out there, aren't they Mr. Bryson? But I know I can't play goal. I don't even want to try."

I stopped talking. I would rather have to spend every game on the bench than to face those flying pucks, especially ones sent by kids who didn't like East Indians in the first place. There was no way I was going to play goal and give everyone a chance to shoot pucks at me, even if it was only a game!

"Listen Ron," said Mr. Bryson. "You've got good flexibility and your reflexes are quick and accurate. That's where your strength is, not in your skating. With a little experience you'll do fine as a goalie. In the meantime, you can keep working on your skating so that next year you can play another position if you want to."

He looked at me for a minute, then smiled. It was one of his tight smiles, the ones that didn't look as if he meant them. I thought he looked nervous and wondered what he was working himself up to say.

"The whole team depends on their goalie," he said. "In many ways he is the most important player we have. It would be good for you to take that position, good for your...uh...relationship with the others. Once you prove to them, and to yourself, that you can do well in goal, I think you'll find that things are more comfortable for you on the team."

"You mean they'll forget I'm not white?" I asked, immediately hating myself for saying it. "Sorry, Coach, I guess I didn't quite mean that."

"It's all right, Ron. Yes, I admit that there is a certain degree of uncomfortableness among the other team members. But they're trying, Ron. We're all trying. I know you'll be a good goalie and I also know it will help the rest of the team get to know you. Give yourself a chance. Give them a chance, too."

I had my mouth open to answer the coach, to tell him that there was no way I'd play goal, when the door to the dressing room burst open and Big Bill from the registration booth stormed in.

"Les, what in blazes is keeping you? I've been waiting twenty minutes."

"Sorry, Dad." Les lowered his head and stared at the floor again.

Dad. I guess I should have realized that Big Bill would turn out to be Les' father. Now that I saw them together, I could see the resemblance.

"We're nearly finished, Mr. Johnson," said the coach. "We've just been discussing what position the boys will play this year. Les is going to be defense."

"Defense? But he's the goalie."

"We're making a few changes this season. Les has spent two seasons in the net and it's time he got out of there and worked on strengthening his other skills. He'll play a strong defense for the team."

"No, he won't. He's staying in goal."

"Well, we can discuss it further if you like, but the decision has been made. Ron is taking over the goalie spot this year."

Bill Johnson looked directly at me for the first time. "Him? The Hindu? He can't even skate."

"Ron will be a good goalie once he's had a bit of experience. I'm sorry you're upset, Mr. Johnson, but I think Les needs a change."

"We'll see about that!" Bill Johnson's face was red, mottled with white. I hoped he wasn't going to have a heart attack. Mr. Bryson stood up quickly and took Mr. Johnson's arm.

"Settle down, Bill," he said, steering him into a corner of the room, away from me and Les. "Take it easy, will you?"

When Mr. Johnson spoke again, he sounded as if he were choking. The coach lowered his voice so that Les and I couldn't hear, but Mr. Johnson didn't even try.

"We'll see what the division head has to say about that, Bryson. You've got no right to pull my son out of a position he's good at just to give some Hindu a chance to play. I'll fight you over this; fight you all the way up to the executive of the league."

Right then was when I decided that I would play goal. Mr. Bill Johnson could call me all the names he wanted, but I was going to be the team's goalie, the best goalie they'd ever had in Dinway's minor hockey league.

The coach and Les' father were still talking in the corner of the room.

"I'm sorry you feel that way Bill," I heard Mr. Bryson say. "I can assure you that Les agrees with me that it's time he moved to another position. Right, Les?"

"It doesn't matter what Les thinks, Bryson. He's the goalie of this team and he's going to stay the goalie."

"I'll be glad to discuss this with you or with the executive if you prefer," said Mr. Bryson. "But not right now. Or right here." He glanced over his shoulder at us. "I have to leave. Les, Ron, I'll see you Wednesday for our first game."

The coach left the dressing roon and I grabbed my equipment bag and followed him. As fast as I could.

I didn't want to stay in the same room as the Johnsons any longer than I had to. Besides, I wanted to catch up to Mr. Bryson and tell him that he'd found himself a new goalie.

Les and his father were alone in the dressing room and as the door shut behind me, I could hear their voices. Bill Johnson's voice was loud—loud and angry—but it didn't quite cover the thin sound of someone beginning to cry.

6

I don't remember much about that first game, except Coach Bryson's words to me before it began. "Keep your eye on the puck and your stick on the ice and you'll do fine." I didn't do "fine," but I guess I did okay. It seemed that most of the action took place around the other net where my team was pushing hard, so there weren't too many shots sent my way by the other team. Somehow or other I made a few saves and only let three goals through.

But Les was right. It was frightening in goal. I felt alone out there, crouched down in the net, waiting and watching. Then, when the play did move to our end, it seemed as if everyone was tearing down the ice, right at me. Once or twice I almost ducked as a shot came my way, instead of going for it the way I knew I was supposed to. I could see why Les was willing to get out of goal. After two years of this, it was surprising that he hadn't quit hockey completely!

It wasn't just the fast shots that made being in the net so difficult. I had never worn full goalie equipment before and sometimes I found it almost impossible to move. The goalie equipment all belonged to the league, except for the face mask which I had bought myself.

The trapper had molded itself to fit someone else's hand, not mine. It felt tight and uncomfortable and pinched my little finger. The knee pads were so wide that they rubbed together as I skated and so bulky that when I fell down (sometimes to stop a shot, but more often just by accident) I couldn't get up very quickly. And something seemed to be wrong with my skates. Whenever I tried to move sideways, they'd catch on the ice and I'd stumble.

Coach Bryson had said that from now on I'd be doing all the skating drills at practice in full equipment. He warned me that the goalie's equipment took some time to get used to, but I hadn't expected anything like this.

I tried, though, I really did. Once or twice I found myself shutting my eyes as the puck flew towards me, afraid that if I kept on looking at it I'd get hit. I guess no one noticed that my eyes were shut; the wire mask pretty well covered my face. At least, I hoped no one noticed.

Near the end of the game however, the tangle of players and sticks and puck began to sort itself out and I could almost figure out what was going on. The knee pads were still awkward and the trapper still hurt my finger, but I began to think that maybe I'd be able to handle playing goal.

The parents went wild during the game. There seemed to be a half-dozen spectators for every player on the ice, all of them excited because it was the first game of the season. They all shouted more often, and more loudly, than they had at practices.

"Skate, Brian, skate!" I heard them yell at our centre. Or "Go for it, Legion!" "Check him, Robin! Get on him." Near the end of the game I managed to catch a shot in my trapper and I heard someone in the bleachers yell out, "Nice save, Ron. Well done!"

Hearing that made me feel peculiar. It was nice of someone else's dad to cheer for me, but my parents weren't there to watch. My real name isn't "Ron," either and my mom and dad wouldn't shout "Well done." They'd call out "shabash!" which is a Punjabi word which means about the same thing—well done, good work.

For a moment after I heard my name called I felt very alone. I strained my ears, listening hard, hoping to hear someone call "Shabash, Rana, shabash!" Then I realized how dumb that was. My family would never come to a hockey game. As my father had said, it was a game for the gorays, the whites. I had better learn to appreciate a shout of "Well done, Ron!" because "Shabash, Rana!" was the last thing I'd ever hear at one of my hockey games.

I turned my attention back to what was happening on the ice, pushing away the lonely feeling. Just in time, too. One of the other team's wings scooted around the back of the net and shot. I lunged at the puck with my stick and missed, but my skate caught it, sending it out of the net. "Go goalie, go!" someone shouted and there was a smattering of applause. I forgot about feeling lonely, and concentrated on the rest of the game.

We almost let them tie us. We were ahead, four to three and the clock was running out when their centre broke away, raced towards me, and shot. I reached out too soon with my stick, lost my balance, and fell flat on my stomach. The buzzer sounded and everyone shouted and cheered.

I lay on the ice, wondering what we did about tie games, ashamed to get up and face my team.

But the spectators were still shouting, "Way to go, Legion!" and my team-mates were lifting their sticks in the air and cheering. Brian, our centre, skated up to the net.

"Get up, Ron. Come on. We've got to go and shake hands with the other team. We won!"

"But..." I said, looking around behind me for the puck.

"But that last shot went in. We tied."

"No way it went in," said Brian. "You fell on it. Stopped it dead."

I lifted my stomach off the ice and looked. There was the puck, safe. We had won.

"Hey," I said. "How about that?"

I was changed and ready to go home, the goalie equipment stored away in the team's locker and my own stuff packed in my gym bag, when Les came over to me.

Everyone else had left the dressing room. I was feeling sick to my stomach, which was why it had taken me longer than usual to change. I didn't know why Les was still hanging around. He was usually one of the first out of there.

"Um..." he said. "Um, I...."

Not now, I thought. I was tired and my muscles ached. My hand hurt where the trapper had pinched it and I thought I might throw up. I was in no mood for a fight. If Les started telling me what I'd done wrong in the goal, I'd have to stand up and plow him one, and I didn't feel like it.

"What do you want?" I said, almost shouting. "You going to lend me your helmet or something?"

He blushed—he actually blushed—the red stain creeping down his neck. He pulled at the collar of his T-shirt and coughed.

Come on lard ass, I said to myself. *So you don't like East Indians? Well I don't like fat people. If you're pushing for a fight, let's get on with it.*

"Yeah...well, no...I mean...." Les had run out of words again, but by now I could tell that he wasn't angry, that he wasn't going to start calling me names, wasn't looking for a fight. What did he want, then? I didn't have a clue.

"Sorry, " I said. "I didn't mean that about the helmet. I'm wiped and I don't feel great. I need to go home and shower and get something to eat, if my stomach will let me."

"Here." Les fished around in his equipment bag and brought out a chocolate bar. "I always have something sweet after a game," he said. "You know, coach says it brings your energy level back up." He held out the chocolate bar, offering it to me.

I was too surprised to do anything but take it, then I sat there and stared at the bar in my hand as if I'd never seen one before.

"Go ahead," said Les. "I've got another one. He dug around in his bag again and came up with another chocolate bar, unwrapped it and stuffed half of it into his mouth. I unwrapped mine and took a small bite, wondering if I could handle it or if I were going to throw it right back up.

"Um...I think..." Les chewed, swallowed, then the words came out in a rush. "I think you did okay in the net today and I'm sorry for what my dad said about you and I'm sure glad I don't have to play in goal any more."

It was my turn not to know what to say. "Um...yeah, thanks," I mumbled.

"Wereyouscared?" Again his words rushed out, so fast they all ran together. And I understood why he had stayed behind, had shared his chocolate bars with me. He wanted to find out if it was just him who was scared playing goal. For a minute I considered telling him that I didn't know what he'd found so frightening, that I hadn't thought it the least bit terrifying, that I'd been cool and calm the whole time.

Then I looked at the way his eyes seemed almost to be pleading with me and decided to level with him.

"I've never been so scared in my life! Half the time I fell down out there, it wasn't on purpose to cover the puck, it was just because my legs wouldn't hold me up." I swallowed and looked down at the candy bar in my hand, wishing I hadn't tried to eat any of it. "And right now I think I'm going to barf."

"Yeah," said Les and he smiled and his eyes lost the begging look I'd seen in them. "Yeah, I figured it was getting to you. I saw you shut your eyes once and miss a shot. That's how they got that second goal."

"I know," I said. "But right now I don't care. I've got to get out of here, get some fresh air."

Les followed me to the door, talking the whole time. He'd had trouble starting this conversation, but now he wasn't shutting up.

"I used to get the same way, but before the game, not after. Once I did throw up. Lots of goalies do."

"Lots of goalies do what? Barf? You're joking."

"Nope. There's this real famous goalie. Glenn Hall. He always took a pail with him to the bench and sometimes he had to use it. Right there. In front of everyone."

"Glenn who?"

Les looked at me as if I'd spoken in Punjabi instead of English. "You don't know who Glenn Hall is? Really? He played for the Blues and the Black Hawks for years. He's retired now, but everyone knows about him. He was a great goalie, but it used to make him sick."

"How do you know all of that?" I asked.

"My dad. He got me these books about hockey and one of them is all about goalies. It's got some good stuff in it."

"Good stuff? Guys barfing into pails? Yeah, right!"

"No, really, it's interesting," Les said. He took the last bite of his chocolate bar and tucked the wrapper into his pocket. "I could...I mean, if you want to you can borrow the book."

I thought for a minute. Reading about other goalies, professional players—grown-up men, who were so scared they barfed before they went into the net—might not be such a bad idea after all. I felt better already. It wasn't that big a deal to feel nervous, not if all these other goalies felt that way too.

"Great," I said. "I don't know much about hockey, but

that book sounds okay. Might learn some things about playing goal, too."

"If you got your skates sharpened the right way you wouldn't have so much trouble," Les said.

"I got them sharpened before the game," I said.

"Yeah, but they sharpen goalies' skates a different way, more on the edges. So you can move sideways better."

"I didn't know that," I said, remembering how my skates had seemed to catch on the ice when I'd tried to go sideways.

"I guess Coach forgot to tell you," said Les. "You can get them done for the next game and it will help."

"I need all the help I can get," I said. "Thanks."

We went out the arena's side door and the first breath of cold air fixed my stomach for good. I felt okay again. Felt hungry, as a matter of fact.

"Hey! Snow!" Les and I stared up into the thick, grey sky, feeling the cold feathers of the first snow brush against our faces.

"It's early this year," I said. "That's great. I love it when it snows."

"Really? I thought all...all of you people liked the hot weather like it is in India and didn't like the cold."

I laughed. "That's just some of the older ones, Les. They miss India and miss the climate there. Me, I was born here. This is my kind of weather."

"Me too. Not enough for snowballs, though. My dad said it was going to snow. That's why he didn't come to the game. Went to get the snow tires put on the truck."

"Is your dad still mad? Because you're not goalie?" It was hard to ask that question, but I wanted to know the answer. If Big Bill were still shouting about Hindus taking his son's position on the hockey team, then maybe I'd better not borrow anything from Les.

Les thought for a bit. "Well, he was a bit upset at first. Yeah, you know that, you were there. But he says maybe

I'll lose some weight now that I'm moving around more during games and practices. He doesn't like me being fat."

"But, he...." I started to say something, then shut my mouth in a hurry. No point in reminding Les that his father and mother weren't exactly skinny.

"I bet I can too," he said. "Lose weight, I mean. I hate it when the kids call me names. This year the girls have started with "gross-o." Last year it was "fat ass" and "slob" and they make pig noises when I eat my lunch."

"Yeah." I tried to smile. "Yeah, I know what you mean."

Les blushed again. "I guess you do," he said. "I guess you know what it feels like when people dump on you."

"Doesn't bother me any more," I lied. Then I changed the subject. I didn't want to think about what I'd nearly called Les when I thought he was only hanging around after the game to fight with me. "Lard-ass." It wasn't the same as "stinking Hindu" but I wasn't proud of myself for thinking it.

"You live around here?" I asked.

"Two blocks up and three over."

"I'm up that way, too. Let's go. How come you don't go to my school?"

"I used to. My dad, he said the teachers were slacking off and that's why I wasn't doing so good. He made me go to another school, but I'm still not doing great. Especially in math. I hate math."

"Me, too." I said. I didn't mention that I almost always got As in math. I didn't like it much, that was true.

We talked all the way up the hill, until Les turned right and I turned left, heading home.

"See ya, Ron," he called. "I'll bring that book to the next practice."

"Sure, see you soon," I said. And I really wanted to.

7

Things went well for the next few games. I didn't get any shut-outs or anything, but our team was winning and I was one of the reasons we won. I was learning how to be a goalie, a good one.

The whole team was pleased with me, with themselves. After a game they'd thump me on the helmet, grinning and congratulating me. Everyone talked to me in the dressing room now, things like, "Hey, where was the ref? That guy should have had about 20 penalties." Or, "Some save on that slapshot, Ron. Way to go!"

Coach Bryson was pleased with me, too. "You're doing just fine, Ron," he'd say. "I knew you'd be a good goalie. Keep up the good work!"

I was proud of myself. The funny, sick-to-my-stomach feeling that I got during games and afterwards was still there, and I'd have times when I wanted to shut my eyes and duck a shot instead of trying to stop it, but on the whole I thought I was doing okay. More than okay, really. I guess I was pretty pleased with myself. I should have known better.

There's a saying I read in some book at school; "Pride goes before a fall." During my thirteenth game as goalie, I just "fell" apart. Maybe thirteen is an unlucky number; it sure seemed that way to me.

I couldn't seem to do anything right in the net. I started missing the puck, losing it, moving out of the crease at the wrong time and even tripping over my own feet. It wasn't the way my skates were sharpened either, it was just me. I could only stop the easiest, slowest shots and the other teams all won with high scores. As the weeks went on, the bad luck that began with the thirteenth game didn't end, either. It seemed to get worse. I began to wonder if I were invisible, because the puck seemed to be going right through me at times. A lot of times.

After a few of the bad games, Coach Bryson took me aside. "Don't worry Ron," he said. "You've had to learn too much too quickly. All the new skills are there, but you're using your brain too much, worrying about what you're supposed to be doing."

"No," I said, "I'm worried about what I'm *not* doing. Stopping the shots."

"You've got to stop sweating it, Ron. It's making it even worse. Start thinking with your body, not with your mind. Your reflexes have slowed down because your mind keeps on telling them what to do, instead of letting them work on their own, the way they're supposed to."

"I don't know, Coach. Maybe Les should take over for a while," I said, hating myself for saying it because I knew that there was no way that Les would go back in that net.

"No," the coach reassured me. "No, I don't think replacing you with Les is the answer, for either of you. Everything will come together for you again, and you'll be a better goalie than you were before. I have faith in you Ron."

He may have had faith in me, but my belief in myself

had vanished.

Instead of boosting my spirits with his pep talk, the coach had made me feel worse. I felt as if I were letting him down, as well as the rest of my team.

We lost game after game and I felt worse and worse. And I learned something that I didn't particularly want to know—no matter how rotten the rest of the team is, no matter how badly they play, they blame the *goalie* if they lose. The others forget about their penalties, their bad skating, their mistakes, but they remember every shot the goalie lets through.

The rest of my team, who had been friendly and encouraging when we were winning, began to avoid me again. They'd turn their backs when I came into the dressing room and I'd hear comments fly around the room. Not just comments on my lousy performance in goal, but some of the other kind too. The "stinking Hindu" or "rag-head" type of thing. No one dared say anything like that around the coach though, and I don't think he realized how bad things were getting for me. I wasn't about to tell him, either.

It was only because of Les that I was able to keep going, to keep showing up for practices and games. We'd walk home together after practices and sometimes after games, if his dad wasn't there. Les loaned me all kinds of books about hockey and I read everything he gave me. The books didn't help me improve, but I learned a lot.

Les knew about being goalie, about having to take the blame for the team losing games. "Don't worry, Ron," he told me after a particularly humiliating game where we'd lost ten to one. "Don't let it get to you. The guys need someone to blame and the goalie is the best person around to take all the garbage."

He reached over and punched me lightly on the shoulder. "Hey," he said, "They don't really mean it, what they're saying about you. Every time we lost a few games last year, they'd start calling me names too. Fat names. The team has got to have a reason for losing, you know. My dad said that. Last year the reason was that I was too fat; this year it's because you're East Indian. Don't sweat it, okay?"

I tried not to sweat it, but it really got to me. I began hanging around outside the dressing room after a game, not going in to change until most of my team had left. Then I'd rush in, change in a hurry and get out of there as fast as I could.

One set of lockers was in the back of the room, angled so that it jutted out and made a private space behind it. I'd head for this corner and change there, hoping that no one would say anything to me about the game we'd just lost. Actually, no one but Les wanted to talk to me at all and I didn't have much to say to them, either. How many times can you apologize, anyway? And it wasn't all my fault, but no one but me seemed to accept that.

I was back in that blocked-off space behind the lockers one Saturday, the only player except for Les who hadn't gone home. The coach was there, making sure things were tidy and the league's equipment was locked up before he took off. I don't think the coach knew I was still there and I didn't feel like talking to anyone, not even Les, so I kept quiet and hoped they'd leave soon so I could get out of there without having to face anyone.

Les and Mr. Bryson didn't know I was in the dressing room, which is why the whole thing happened. I was quietly stuffing my equipment into my bag when I heard a voice, a loud voice.

"Bryson, I want to talk to you." I didn't need to look around the lockers to see who was speaking—Bill Johnson, Les' father.

"I'm ready, dad," said Les. "I'm coming."

But Mr. Johnson hadn't been waiting for Les. "Get out of here Les," he said. "Go wait in the truck."

"But, Dad...."

"Do what you're told. This isn't your business."

I heard Les leave, grumbling to himself. He slammed the door behind him and I jumped at the noise. Perhaps I should grab my equipment and make tracks out of there myself, but I didn't want to face Big Bill today. Not after the lousy way I'd been playing lately. So I decided to keep quiet. Maybe they wouldn't be long, maybe they'd go somewhere else to talk. I decided to stay quiet and hope no one realized that I was there. A very bad decision.

"Sit down, Mr. Johnson," said the coach.

"I'm not sitting, Bryson. What I got to say is best said standing up."

I heard the coach sigh. "Go ahead then, Mr. Johnson. I'm listening."

"Get that damned Hindu out of goal, Bryson, or I'm pulling my kid off your team. Maybe out of the league. Get him out of there and put Les back where he belongs."

Coach Bryson sighed again before he answered. He sounded tired. "Look, I realize that Ron has had a few bad games, but...."

"A few? You call six losses in a row a few?"

"Sure," said the coach. "It's early in the season yet. The team will pull out of this slump."

"It's not the team's fault, Bryson. It's that rag-head you've put in goal." Bill Johnson's voice got louder. I slouched further down on the bench, wishing I'd left the dressing room when I'd had a chance.

Mr. Bryson raised his voice, too. "Mr. Johnson, Ron has shown excellent sportsmanship and a good potential for hockey. This is his first year in the league, but he's learning fast and I believe he is this team's best choice for goalie. And I'd say that about him no matter what his race. The fact that he's an East Indian has nothing to do with my choosing him as goalie, or the fact that he's had some bad games recently."

"Bull! Everyone knows those Hindus are poor sports. They can't play hockey, or much of anything except cricket. Get him out of there, Bryson, get him out now! I'm warning you. I'll pull my kid off the team and take as many others with me as I can. Get him out of the net."

I could feel my cheeks burning and my hands beginning to tremble. I'd had about all I could take, first from my team-mates and now from Mr. Bill Johnson. I stood up, straightened my ghuta, took a deep breath and walked out from behind the lockers that hid me from their view.

But the door to the dressing room flew open, slamming back against the wall, and no one turned to look at me.

"Dad, you can't make the coach do that! You can't!"

It was Les. He must have stayed just outside the door to listen, instead of going to the truck as his father had told him to do.

"Ron is a good goalie," he went on. "Better than me. And I won't play goal again. I won't!"

"Shut your mouth, Les. I'll deal with you when we get home."

"I don't care what you do to me. I'm not going to play goal, never again. I hate it, hate it...and I'm scared. Ask the coach. That's why he pulled me. I'm no good in goal any more because I'm scared."

There was silence when Les finished. No one had seen me yet, although I was out of my hiding place, in full view if they'd turn around and look. The silence stretched on and then Bill Johnson spoke again, as if Les hadn't said anything at all.

"My son will play goal, Bryson. I'll see to that. It's bad enough that I lost my job to one of them, but I won't have my son losing his position on the team to a stinking Hindu as well. You just change your goalies, before your whole team quits on you."

"It's all right, coach," I said. "Don't worry about pulling me out of the net. You gorays can have your stupid hockey team. I quit!"

Before they had a chance to say anything, I went for the door. I had to cross in front of all three of them, and I did it quickly, wanting to get out of there as soon as I could. I wanted to get out of the whole hockey thing as soon as I could. Les was looking at me with his mouth hanging open and Bill Johnson was red in the face again. Coach Bryson shook his head at me, but he didn't say anything.

I knew they were all staring, but I didn't care. Just as I reached the door, before I stepped out of the room, I turned around and said something in Punjabi. It's a good thing my parents didn't hear what I said, or I would have been grounded for a month. But Fat Bill didn't speak Punjabi, so he'd never know what I had called him.

I switched back to English. "Take your stupid game and shove it," I said. "Just shove it."

8

I don't remember walking home that day. I was so angry that I hardly knew what I was doing. Once a car braked and honked at me and I realized that I'd walked out in front of it, not looking, not caring.

I was sorry I had lost my temper. No, I wasn't, not really. My parents are very strict about swearing, in Punjabi or English and they insist that kids show respect for adults. But Bill Johnson didn't deserve my respect. I'd had enough—enough listening to the team blame me for losing games, enough trying to keep smiling, pretending I hadn't heard the comments in the dressing room. And I'd had more than enough of Mr. Bill Johnson. Les was okay, but his father was something else. Something rotten.

Dinner was ready when I got home.

I ate, not saying much, hoping my parents wouldn't ask about the game.

"Rana?" My mother looked worried. "Is everything all right? You are so quiet. Are you sick?"

Everyone looked at me.

"He looks okay to me," said Babli. "Just as dumb as he always does." She giggled.

"Hush, Babli. Rana? Tell me, what is wrong?"

"Maybe he's being a bridge again," said Babli. "Bridges don't talk."

"Enough, Babli." My father turned to me. "Rana? Answer your mother. Are you ill?"

"No," I said, swallowing a mouthful of roti. My throat was dry and I had to take a drink of milk before I could finish answering my dad. "No, I'm not sick, Dad. Everything's fine. We lost another game, that's all."

"Ah. The hockey. I understand," he said.

But he didn't understand and I wasn't about to tell him. Sooner or later I'd have to tell them that I'd quit the team but not yet. I knew that they'd be disappointed in me. Especially my mom, who had stood up for me when my dad hadn't wanted me to join. And even my father, who'd been so against me joining in the first place, was busy telling everyone at the temple about his son who played minor hockey. His son who was the goalie.

Who *had been* the goalie. I wasn't ready to tell my parents about my quitting, I wasn't ready to talk to anyone about it. I hoped my friends wouldn't ask about hockey this Sunday at temple. A group of us always hung around and talked after the worship service was over and some of the guys were really interested in the games. I wondered if they would have heard about my quitting; what if someone asked me how things were going? I was too upset, too churned up inside, to want to talk about it.

Mom and Babli had just finished clearing the table when the doorbell rang. "I'll get it," Babli called and bounced off down the stairs to the front door.

"Oh!" I heard her say. Someone spoke to her for a moment, then she called to me. "Rana, come down. Your coach is here."

Mr. Bryson? Why was he here? I reluctantly went down

the stairs. I had an idea of what he wanted to say to me, but I didn't want to hear it.

My coach stood on the front porch, muffled up in his heavy jacket and woollen cap, but wearing runners instead of boots, even though it had been snowing. I opened my mouth, hoping I could tell him something quickly so he'd go away before my parents found out he was here, but no words came out.

"Ron, can I come in please?" he said. "I'd like to talk to you."

"Maybe we could go outside and talk?" I said, grabbing my boots. "Let's talk out there." But it was too late. Babli had been hanging over the stair railing, her eyes wide.

I looked up and saw that my mother and father had joined her. They were all standing at the head of the stairs, watching me.

"Come in, please," said my father. "Rana, bring your coach upstairs. Why this talk of outside? It is snowing."

"Hello," said my mother, in English, smiling. "Hello. Come, please." She smiled again.

I saw Mr. Bryson look up the stairs at my parents and I saw him blink. Once, twice.

Nervous as I was about why he had come to see me, I looked behind me to see what had surprised him.

"Thank you, Mr. Bains, Mrs. Bains," he said, but he wasn't looking at my parent's faces, just at their feet. More specifically, at my mother's feet. Both mom and dad were barefoot and so was I. But mom was wearing her toe rings tonight; small gold rings that she'd been given on her wedding day. Regular rings, but made to fit toes, not fingers. I'd never thought about it much, but I guess most mothers in Dinway don't wear rings on their toes.

"Come upstairs, please," my father said again, then spoke to my mother in Punjabi, telling her to go and make a pot of chai, sweet milky tea with spices.

"Uh, Ron?"

Coach Bryson had taken off his jacket and I took it from him and hung it up in the hall closet. "Ron?" he said again and his voice was funny, much weaker than it usually was.

"Come upstairs then," I said. "Everyone seems to want to see you."

"Shall I take off my shoes?" he asked. "I see your mom and dad aren't wearing any."

I shrugged.

"If you want to. It's not a rule, except in the temple, but Mom's real fussy about her carpets."

"Oh." He bent down to unlace his runners and I realized that he was nervous. Good. That made two of us. I knew why I was worried at seeing him here, but what was wrong with the coach?

"Ron, it seems stupid to say this, but I've never been in an East Indian home. Please tell me if I'm breaking some of your rules or something."

I had to grin. "Don't worry, Coach. We've never had a white person in our home before. Mom and Dad are probably more nervous than you are."

The coach took off his shoes, but left his socks on. He didn't need to show off his toes, I guess. Probably didn't go in much for toe rings.

We went upstairs. "Mom, Dad, this is Mr. Bryson, my coach," I said formally, even though they knew perfectly well who he was.

My father folded his hands and bowed his head.

"Sat sri akal," he said. "Welcome to our home."

"Hello, hello," said my mother again, from the kitchen door.

"My wife will bring us tea, Mr. Bryson. Are you hungry?"

"Uh, no, I've eaten, thank you. And I can't stay for tea, but thank you just the same. I only have a few minutes and I need to talk to Ron. If you don't mind."

"I see. Perhaps you will come another time and drink

tea with us? But for now you want to speak to Rana alone, yes? About the hockey?"

"Yes," said Coach Bryson. "The hockey. Ron's hockey."

"Very well. We will leave the two of you together so you may settle this hockey matter."

I watched my family go down the stairs to the basement room and heard the TV being turned on. I know Babli didn't want to go; she kept looking at me and the coach. I hoped Mom would keep a close eye on her, otherwise she'd probably sneak back and listen to our conversation. And I didn't want Babli to hear what the coach had to say to me about my quitting the team. That was something I'd have to tell my parents myself and, thanks to Mr. Bryson's visit, I'd have to tell them sooner than I'd wanted to. My dad was being polite, but I knew he was as curious as Babli. There would be a lot of questions to answer once Coach Bryson left.

"Might as well get it over with," I thought. I took a deep breath.

"I'm sorry I lost my temper today. I should have left as soon as I heard Mr. Johnson's voice, but...."

"Yes, you should have done that," said Mr. Bryson. "Eavesdropping isn't a nice habit."

"I didn't mean to eavesdrop," I said. "It was an accident. I was just trying to stay out of everyone's way, so I wouldn't have to talk to them."

"I wondered if that was why you were hiding back there."

"I wasn't hiding!"

"Okay Ron, relax. Perhaps you didn't mean to overhear that conversation; perhaps you weren't intentionally staying out of sight. That's not really the problem, is it?"

"I don't have a problem," I said. "Mr. Johnson does. A prejudice problem."

"I agree," the coach said. "He owes you an apology and I hope he'll offer it to you."

"I don't care if he does," I said. "I don't want to see him ever again. Or hear his Hindu comments."

"What Mr. Johnson feels about you doesn't really matter," said the coach.

"Get real!" I said. "Sir."

"And don't start with the 'sir' garbage, Ron. Get off your high horse for long enough to think about someone else for a change. Stop feeling sorry for yourself."

I was too surprised to answer him. Mr. Bryson had always been supportive of me; I'd never heard him talk like this. I wasn't on a "high horse" whatever that meant. Sure, I was feeling sorry for myself, but I had a right to do that. Didn't I?

"It doesn't matter what anyone says about your playing, Ron. That's the game; that's sports. Every couch potato in the world feels that they have a right to criticize the players, in the minor leagues as well as in professional leagues. Once you go out there on the ice, you're public property. Or your performance is. It may not be fair, but it's how things work."

"I don't understand," I said. "You're telling me that Mr. Johnson has a right to call me a lousy rag-head?"

"No, he doesn't. But he does have a right to comment on your ability to play hockey. And my ability to coach it."

"He did that, all right," I said.

"But you don't have the right to quit the team."

"What?" I said. "That's not fair, coach. He can call me names and I can't do anything but hang around and take it?"

"Mr. Johnson's prejudice is another matter, Ron. Your poor sportsmanship is what we're talking about here."

"Poor sportsmanship? Me?"

"Yes. You are our goalie. You're an important member of our team. If you walk away now, you're punishing every player on that team for your temper."

I was confused. "But I'm right to be upset by what he

said about me. How come it's my fault all of a sudden?"

The coach smiled. "It seems backwards, doesn't it? I'm lecturing you about team loyalty and sportsmanship because of Bill Johnson's mean mouth. What I'm trying to say to you Ron, is that if you let yourself quit the team now, you are as wrong as Mr. Johnson is. You're letting us all down; the rest of the team and me."

"You? But I've worked hard for you, coach. I've tried."

"Yes, Ron. And I've tried. I've stuck my neck out for you from the moment I heard you were trying to register. I made sure you'd be on my team; I've pushed the others to accept you; I've been strict about racist language. I worked hard to make your experience with minor hockey a positive one. If you walk away, you let the team down and you let me down. I had faith in you, Ron. Part of learning to play any sport is learning how to lose as well as to win and I thought you could deal with that. Maybe I was wrong. I never believed you would be a quitter."

"I'm not," I said, before I realized what I was saying.

Mr. Bryson smiled again. "I know that, Ron. But I'm very glad to hear you say it. Welcome back to the team."

"But, I...." I began, then stopped. *How had that happened?* I wondered. Five minutes ago I had sworn off hockey for life and now here I was back in the league. I thought about what the coach had said and of all the dumb things, I thought about Mom's bridge. How she said that hockey would be a bridge between my world and the other world. The white world, the Canadian world.

I didn't want to leave hockey. Forget about the bridge; I liked playing, liked the practices, liked being on the team. Except when we lost. Maybe you never learned to like losing, but as Mr. Bryson said, you had to learn to deal with it. It was all part of the game.

"Okay," I said. "I'm back."

"You never really left, Ron. I wasn't going to let you take the easy way out by quitting."

"But keep Mr. Johnson away from me, okay?" I said.

"There's something else you should know, Ron. There's a special meeting of the minor league executive tonight; I'm on my way there now. It's time we faced the issue of prejudice and dealt with it. You kids don't just learn hockey; you learn to work as a team, to share, to co-operate. You learn the meaning of the word 'sportsmanship,' and that is more important than all the skating techniques you could ever learn. Parents like Mr. Johnson are undermining the purpose of the minor hockey league; racism has no place on the ice."

"You mean, this meeting is about what happened with me and him? The other parents are standing up for me?"

"Yes. Although I shouldn't be telling you this, Ron, I'm sure we won't have any more trouble with Mr. Johnson, not after tonight."

My father came up the stairs, looking worried. "I don't want to interrupt, Mr. Bryson, but I hope that there is nothing wrong. That Rana has not made problems for you."

"No, Mr. Bains, no problems. A small misunderstanding which Ron and I have cleared up." The coach looked at me, then back at my father. "Ron will tell you about it himself. When he is ready to."

I couldn't meet my father's questioning eyes. I wasn't ready to talk about it.

"I have to go now," said Mr. Bryson. "I have a meeting in a few minutes."

"Rana will see you to the door," said my father. "I hope you will visit us again, Mr. Bryson. Perhaps next time you will stay and eat with us, if you are fond of spicy food."

"Sounds good," said the coach. "I've never tried East Indian food, but I'd like to. I'll probably like it, because I love Mexican food and it's hot."

"We look forward to having you here. Please do come."

My father folded his hands and bowed. "Sat sri akal," he said.

The coach looked puzzled. "I don't understand," he said.

"It's a greeting, a ceremonial sort of thing," I said. "It means 'True is the Lord,' but Sikhs use it to say 'hello,' 'good-bye,' or 'welcome.'"

"Oh, I understand." Mr. Bryson turned to my father, folded his hands and bowed. "Sat sri akal," he said. "Is that okay for me to do? I'm not Sikh, but I thought...."

"Yes. Thank you, Mr. Bryson," said my dad.

"No, thank you for having me in your home and for encouraging Ron to play hockey. He's a strong addition to the team. And he's not a quitter."

I shut the door behind him and turned around to find the whole family staring at me.

"Are you in trouble, Rana?" asked Babli. "What did you do? Won't they let you play hockey any more? Was your coach mad? I bet you're in real trouble, aren't you?"

"Babli, be quiet." Mom looked worried as she spoke. "So," she said. "There is trouble. Your father was right after all."

"Is there trouble Rana?" My father's voice was stern. "Will you tell us why the coach was here?"

I thought for a moment before I answered.

"No, Dad. It's nothing I can't handle. It's just that bridge of Mom's. It's turning out to be harder to build than I figured it would be. Much harder."

My mother smiled. "You will do it, Rana. I know."

I hoped she was right.

9

It was really weird. As soon as I made up my mind to keep fighting, not to quit hockey, things got better. Better with the rest of the team and better on the ice, too. In the dressing room before the next game, Les came over to me.

"I'm sorry, Ron," he said formally. "About what my Dad said. He lost his job at the mill last year, and they gave it to an East Indian man, and he's been real down on you people ever since. But he didn't have to say that about your playing. You're a good goalie."

"Don't worry about it, Les," I said. "What your dad does isn't your fault."

"I know." Les looked miserable. "But he had no right to say what he did about you. That was ignorant."

"Forget it," I said. "I was mad, but I got over it. Maybe he will, too."

Les looked doubtful. "I hope so. He's kind of hard to live with since he had to go to that executive meeting. I don't know what happened, but he was sure mad when he got home."

Our centre, Brian, interrupted. "You decided to stay with the team, hey? Right on."

I don't know how Brian found out that I had quit the team, but he wasn't the only one who knew. Maybe Les had told them, maybe Mr. Bryson had, but everyone seemed to know about it. Lots of the players spoke to me before the game, nothing important, just, "Hey man, we've still got a goalie!" or "Let's win this one, right?" I was embarrassed. I'd only been off the team for a few hours and I didn't want anyone making a big deal about it. But their words made me feel as if they really would have missed me if I'd quit. As if they needed me.

And when I went out on the ice for that game, I found that everything had come together, just the way the coach said it would. The bulky leg pads which had been so awkward during other games felt as comfortable and easy to move around in as my jeans. The stick seemed like part of my arm; I could move it quickly, accurately. The trapper on my hand didn't pinch anymore, but felt right.

Sure, I still fell down a lot during that game. But most of the time I meant to, and the puck was right underneath me when I fell, not in the net behind me. A couple of times my hand seemed to move by itself and pick a shot out of the air, almost before I saw it coming towards me. It was a good game. We won, four to two, and everyone felt great when it was over, especially me.

Les and I walked home together. He didn't say why his dad wasn't at the game and I didn't ask. But he didn't seem to mind his dad not being there, even though almost everyone else's parents were because it was a Saturday. We talked about our win as we walked, and when we got to the corner where he turns off to head for his house, we stopped and talked some more.

Then he asked, "What are you doing this afternoon?"

"Nothing much," I said. "I did my papers before the game. Maybe I'll give one of our video games a work-out."

Les' eyes lit up. "You've got home video games?" he asked.

"Sure. We've got the whole computer bit. My dad really likes working on it, sort of his hobby."

"I've been asking for a video game for a year, but my dad says they're too expensive, now that he doesn't have a regular job. And he thinks I have better things to do—like practising my skating—than sitting in front of a TV playing games. Besides, he's always watching sports, so I'd never get to use the TV for games."

"We've got a second TV just for the computer stuff and games," I said. "It's an old one but it works so it means I can play almost any time I want to. Unless Dad's using the computer."

"What games have you got?"

"The regular. Pacman, Space Invader and the new one with all the hamburgers."

"Really? You've got Burgertime? That's cool."

I thought for a moment. "You want to come over to my house and have a game?"

We stood there, not saying anything, looking at each other. I had never invited a white friend to my house. I could have, but I just never had. There were lots of reasons why I hadn't, but they didn't seem important any more.

He reached up and scratched his nose. "Um...." he said. "Um...yeah, sure. That would be great. I'll just have to phone home and say I'm visiting...visiting someone."

"Sure." I understood. There was no way that Les could tell his father who he was visiting.

"Let's go, then," I said. "I bet I can beat you at Burgertime. I'm the family champion."

My mothers eyes widened when she saw Les, but his eyes widened even more when he saw her toe rings. "Hey!" he said. "I've never seen rings on toes before. Don't they hurt when you walk? Are they real gold?"

"Yes," I said and Mom smiled at Les.

"Hello, hello," she said. "Come, please."

My father was downstairs, working at the computer.

"Sat sri akal, Les," he said. "I am pleased to meet you. I suppose you and Rana wish to do battle with the tiny hamburgers, right?"

"Yes," I said. "If we can use the TV."

"I am finished," said my dad. "But Les, I warn you, Rana is a vicious opponent, or so his sister says."

Dad went upstairs and Les and I set up the game.

He seemed uneasy at first and I saw his nose wrinkle. He must have been smelling the root ginger, garlic and onions that Mom was cooking with. He saw me looking at him and said, "That smells...uh...different."

"Do you like hot foods?" I asked. "I mean spicy hot, not hot hot."

"Hey Ron, look at me. Can't you tell that I like any kind of food? But my mom doesn't cook much and I've never smelled anything like what your mom's making."

From then on, things were fine. We played for an hour or so and I beat him four games out of six. We yelled and shouted while we played and my mother kept poking her head in to see what was going on. Babli came home from her friend's house and came downstairs to watch. She ended up cheering for Les, not for me, and sat there grinning all over her face whenever I made a wrong move.

Then Mom brought food. Cokes and a plateful of her baking. She put the tray down in front of us and spoke to me in Punjabi.

"She says that she thinks you will like these better than the spicy dishes," I translated for Les. "And she says happy eating."

Les looked at the food, then looked at my mother. "Um...thank you. I'll give it a try." Mom smiled at me and she took Babli upstairs with her to help with dinner.

I picked up the plate and passed it to Les. "Go for it," I said.

He looked at the plate for a long moment, then asked, "What are they called?"

"Ledu, for the round cookies. Baysin for the ones that are diamond shaped. They're sweet."

"And those ones? They look like they've got coconut in them."

"They do," I said. "And some spices, but not hot ones."

"What are they called?"

"You don't want to know. Just try it."

"Come on, Ron. What's the name for the coconut stuff?"

"Barfi," I said.

"Really? No way."

"Try one. I'll bet you like it."

"Um...maybe one of these," said Les, reaching out and selecting a ledu.

I watched him as he held it for a moment, then popped the whole thing in his mouth at once, shutting his eyes as he did.

After I had gone upstairs to refill the plate, and that was all gone too, Les leaned back and sighed. "Don't tell my mom that I ate so much," he said. "She's got me on a diet."

"Some diet," I said, remembering how quickly the ledus and baysin and especially the barfi had disappeared.

"Well, I stick to it most of the time. Sort of. How come you don't bring any of this stuff to practice Ron? It's full of quick energy for after a work-out."

I thought about that. "I don't know, Les. Maybe I will."

He left just before supper. My mother invited him to stay, but I think he was still nervous about the spicy food my mom was cooking. Or maybe he was just too full to eat anything else.

"I'd like to, some other time," he said.

"Okay," said Babli. "I'll make the roti when you come. I'm good at that."

"What's roti? Is it like the stuff I had this afternoon?"

Babli wouldn't let him leave after that. She tried to explain what roti was and told him her secret for getting the circles of dough perfectly round and how Golden Temple flour was the best kind to use and a whole bunch of other stuff he didn't want to know. Les was trying to leave, was actually outside the door still listening to Babli chatter at him, when he stuck his head back in. My father and mother were at the head of the stairs just above the front door and Les spoke to them.

"You should come and watch a hockey game sometime, Mr. Bains. I bet you'd like it. You too, Babli and Mrs. Bains. Lots of kids and mothers come, not just the dads."

I think my mother understood what Les said, even though her English isn't good. She must have picked up on the word "hockey," because she smiled and shook her head.

My father didn't smile. He didn't say anything for a while and then he answered seriously. "Perhaps I will, Les. Thank you for inviting me."

It was easy for Les to invite my parents to a hockey game, but I knew they'd never show up at the arena. Babli might want to come to a hockey game sometime, but she'd never dare come by herself; she hadn't even begun to work on her bridge yet.

I had almost destroyed my bridge when I'd tried to quit hockey, but I was glad I hadn't. It was getting stronger and people could cross both ways. Les was the first white friend to cross it, but I went over it every time I went out on the ice with the rest of the hockey team.

But my mother and father would never set foot on that bridge. They were too afraid of getting hurt.

I'd been standing outside the door, watching Les as he left, and I realized my feet were freezing. Bridges! Why was I thinking about that again? Dinner was ready and I was hungry. Never mind about bridges. I wanted to eat.

10

One morning I woke up and it was Christmas. It didn't really happen that suddenly, but that's the way it seemed to me. The decorations and lights had been up in the stores and on houses for a long time and there had been carols on the radio and Christmas movies on the TV for weeks. School had been out for a few days, so I had known that Christmas was coming, but it seemed to sneak up on me and arrive unexpectedly.

Sikhs don't celebrate Christmas the way most of the white community does. It's not a religious time for us, but it is a time for giving gifts and visiting. Some East Indian families put up a tree and decorate their homes, but we never had. Still, we get gifts and we have the holidays, so it's an alright time. I guess the reason that Christmas seemed to arrive without any warning this year was that hockey was taking up more and more of my time and my thoughts. I even had to split my paper route with Babli on the days we had early morning practices. She didn't mind. She liked having the extra money and kept telling me how much she had in the bank and what she was going to buy with it. I didn't really care about the money. Hockey was more important.

I'd been holding down a pretty good record since I came out of my bad spell and we won nearly two games for every one we lost. I was doing well in goal, making saves that just a few months ago, I never could have. The whole team was pleased with the way we were playing. After every game they'd swarm around me, congratulating me and themselves.

Sometimes they got very enthusiastic with their thumps and even though I had my helmet on I was glad of my long hair tied up in its ghuta to help cushion my head.

Les came to visit almost every Saturday. He was getting good with the control stick of the video games. I had to work hard to beat him. Although we spent most of our time playing Burgertime or Pacman, we also talked hockey. Or rather, Les talked and I listened. And learned. His parents had started him in minor hockey when he was five and he watched all the professional games on TV, so he knew everything about the game.

He knew all the teams, the names of the players, their positions, their strengths, their records.

Up to this point I had never watched much hockey on TV. I'd never been interested in sports and no one else in the family was interested either. Even when I joined minor hockey, it was because I enjoyed skating, not because I was a hockey fan.

But one Saturday Les and I sat and watched a hockey game on TV, right from beginning to end. I think I learned more about how hockey is really played that afternoon than I had learned in all the time I'd spent in minor league games and practices.

Les talked all through the game and I tried to see in the plays what he was talking about. He really knew his stuff.

"Watch him," he'd say. "See how he's setting up that shot? Now, keep an eye on Gretzky. See that? He's sneaking in there for a try at goal."

After spending that afternoon with Les, I decided to spend more time watching hockey. I wanted to learn what I could from Canada's best players.

On Boxing Day, Les phoned me. " Hey Ron, you've got to come to my house. I got Centipede for Christmas and Ms. Pacman. Come over and have a game."

I hesitated. Although Les had been to my house often, had even stayed for supper once, I had never visited his home. I wasn't sure that I wanted to go.

Maybe I was still mad at Bill Johnson; mad or maybe a bit scared. I didn't think that Les' father would welcome me to his home and I didn't want to take the chance of being thrown out. Or being called a "stinking Hindu" or something worse.

Come to think of it, I didn't know for sure that Les had ever told his dad that he visited me at my house, that he was friends with one of those "rag-heads."

"Um..." I said at last. "Is your dad home?"

"No one's here but me," said Les. "They've gone off to an open house or some sort of afternoon party. They'll be gone for hours."

"Okay, then. Sure. I'll be right there."

"I'll walk over and meet you," said Les. "Get a move on. This Centipede is really excellent!"

We met at the corner where Les goes right and I go left when we walk home together. Les chattered away, not shutting up for a minute, until we reached his house. I didn't say much, just stared down at the snow. I was nervous.

We stopped in front of a large house with a blue pickup truck parked in the carport. "Here we are," he said.

"Come on and...." he began, then stopped talking.

"What's wrong?" I asked.

"My parents. They're home."

"Oh. " I got a cold, tingling feeling in my stomach, the same feeling I always get during a hockey game.

I hadn't seen Mr. Johnson since the day he told the coach to take me out of goal, the day I had sat there in the dressing room listening to him call me names and telling Coach Bryson what a lousy player I was. Suddenly I didn't want to go into Les' house, Centipede or no Centipede.

Les pulled his shoulders back and tried to suck in his stomach. "Come on. It's my house, too. I can have anyone I want come and visit."

"Les, I don't think...." I didn't finish the sentence. What could I say? That I didn't want to see his parents? That I was afraid of Bill Johnson? That maybe I had my own prejudices against fat gorays who hated anyone of another race or colour?

"Come on, Ron," Les said again. "It will be okay." He didn't look as confident as he sounded.

The front door opened and Bill Johnson stood there, a bottle of beer in his hand. "Hey, Les. Too many people at the open house. Couldn't even get a beer, so we came home. What are you doing standing around in the cold, eh?"

Then he noticed me.

We stood still, the three of us, as if we had been turned to stone, just three statues that someone had dropped there. Finally Les spoke. "Ron is...we were just...." was all he could manage to say.

I stuck a smile on my face. "Hello Mr. Johnson," I said.

He looked down at the bottle of beer in his hand and talked to it. "Uh...hello...Ron," he said.

Les seemed to have gotten himself together.

"Dad," he said, "I asked Ron to come over and play Centipede and...."

I interrupted him. "Les, I can't. I'm sorry, I can't."

"Can't what?"

"Go in with you."

He stared at me, hurt. "Come off it," he said. "I go to your house, don't I?"

"That's different," I said. "I can't. I've got to go."

I turned around and started walking home, not saying good-bye, not trying to smile any more.

I wasn't running away, I told myself. I wasn't quitting anything. I just couldn't face Mr. Johnson. I wasn't chicken. Or maybe I was.

Les didn't say good-bye either and I didn't turn around to see if he was looking at me. I walked faster.

So much for stupid bridges, I thought.

I knew that Les was my friend. He had encouraged me through my bad times in goal, lent me books, come to my house, stood up for me against his father. But I hadn't been able to make myself go into his home.

Les had tried to help me cross my bridge, but I was scared.

Do they make chicken-sized bridges?

11

Once I'd got home, I thought about what had happened at Les' house. Then I looked up his number in the phone book and called him. I'd never phoned him before; guess I'd been afraid of his father answering and hanging up on me.

Bill Johnson did answer. I held onto the receiver tightly, so it wouldn't slip out of my sweating hands and said, "Hello, Mr. Johnson. This is Ron Bains. May I speak to Les, please?"

The silence on the other end of the line seemed to go on for a long time. I wondered if Les' father had hung up the receiver, and was just about to hang up myself, when there was a cough and he spoke again.

"Uh...sure," he said. I heard him call, "Les, it's that...it's Ron." He coughed in my ear again. "Les says that I'm a dinosaur. I'm not. You two want to be friends, it's none of my business." There was the sound of footsteps going away, then Les' voice.

"Yeah? What do you want?"

"Les? Hey, I'm sorry."

"It's okay, I guess. I'd probably feel the same way."

Maybe he would, maybe he did understand.

"Les?" I said again.

"Yeah?"

"I will come to your house. When I'm ready."

"You don't have to, if you don't want to."

"Hey, I have to beat you at Centipede, right?"

"Well, you can try. I've been practising."

There was silence again, then I asked, "Dinosaur?"

"Yeah, well. You know." Les sounded embarrassed. "You see, after you left I told my dad that people like him were dinosaurs, becoming extinct without even the brains to realize it. I said that racism was the cause of the last war and people like him were doing their best to bring on a nuclear holocaust because they wouldn't even try to accept people who were different from them."

"Uh, sure," I mumbled, wondering how Les' father had reacted to that. "Dinosaur, right."

Les went on as if he hadn't heard me. "I also said that it was time his generation moved into the modern world, that it was almost 1981 and time they got rid of their prejudices and tried to build a world where everyone could live in peace and it had better happen soon too, before a nuclear bomb blew everyone up and...."

"You said WHAT?"

"I said that he was a dinosaur becoming extinct because...."

"I heard you. I just can't believe you'd say anything like that to your dad."

"I read it in a newspaper," he said. "Sort of memorized it."

"That figures," I said. "I didn't know you knew any big words like 'dinosaur.'"

* * *

Hockey started again, both practices and games, early in the New Year. I found that two weeks away from it hadn't upset my playing too much. I was a bit stiff after the first practice and the goalie leg pads seemed heavier than I remembered, but that was all the trouble I had. The season went on. We won some, lost some. I had good games, but also some bad ones. But the times we lost didn't bother the rest of the team so much any more. "Tough luck, Ron," they'd say. "No one could have stopped that shot. Man, was it moving!"

I discovered *Hockey Night in Canada* on Saturday night and began to watch regularly. Even got some more hockey books from the library and read them. The players, the teams, their records—for someone who had never even seen a hockey game a year ago, I was learning fast. My parents began to laugh at me.

"Hockey, hockey, hockey—that's all we hear now," my mother said one evening.

"Hockey, hockey, hockey," said Babli, imitating her. "Dumb hockey, stupid hockey, garbage hockey. It's dumb to watch it all the time." She made a face at me.

I made one back. "That's what you think," I said. "What do you know, anyway? You're only in Grade 3."

But when my father began complaining that he never got to watch what he wanted to on TV any more, I realized that I was becoming a hockey addict.

One Saturday night my dad came downstairs while I was watching the game. He settled himself in the big armchair with a plate of pappadam to munch on. I reached out to help myself, not taking my eyes from the screen.

"Wait," said my father. "Not the whole plate." He broke one of the large rounds in half and passed it to me. I prefer chips to pappadam, but tonight I felt like something with more flavour. Pappadam looks like a thin, crunchy pancake and Mom puts it in the microwave to crisp it, although it used to be made in the oven before people had microwaves. It's crunchy and salty and sometimes there's garlic in it or crushed red peppers.

"Since there never seems to be anything but hockey on our TV any more, I thought I would watch it tonight. Tell me about the game, Rana. "

I grinned, pleased. "Sure, Dad. If you'll get Mom to crisp up some more pappadam."

After that it became a Saturday night ritual—me, Dad, lots of pappadam or popcorn and *Hockey Night in Canada.* Dad learned fast. I gave him some of Les' books and he was quick to pick things up. He'd played soccer back in India, but hadn't even been to watch a soccer game in Canada. It, too, was a game for the gorays, he believed. At least that's the way it was in Dinway.

I found that I was enjoying having Dad watch the games with me. Sometimes Mom and Babli would join us, too. They didn't know anything about hockey at first, but soon picked it up. Babli didn't think hockey was so dumb once she'd seen a few games.

On the evenings when the whole family watched the game, we'd get really noisy, cheering and yelling. "Look at him go," someone would yell.

Or "Shabash, Gretzky, shabash!"

One Saturday in February my team was playing against the team sponsored by Safeway. I hadn't been looking forward to that game. They were a strong team and the last time we'd played them we'd lost, six to zero. They had a centre who hogged the puck, but he was good, almost as good as Brian, our centre. That centre was one of the few players I still heard ugly comments from, especially if I stopped one of his shots on goal. But even with their centre refusing to pass half the time, Safeway scored early in the game and kept on scoring.

But the game wasn't going too badly. I was on top of things, had made some difficult saves and our team was pushing them hard. In the last period we were only two goals behind and the Safeway team wasn't exactly laughing. They'd been walking over every other team in the division lately and I guess they figured we would be easy to beat.

Their centre was getting angry; I could tell. He'd only scored once because I'd managed to block all of his other shots. He was slapping the puck around, not controlling it, just whacking it as hard as he could. He made a shot from behind the centre line that sped towards me. I held up my hand to show the rest of my team's players that it was icing, but he came after it, fast. The whistle blew on the play and he yelled at me. "Watch it. Just watch it, raghead."

"Watch it yourself," I yelled back, cheerfully. I was having a good game and wasn't going to let myself get upset. He slammed his stick down hard before heading back down the ice into the face-off circle.

He grabbed the puck as soon as it was dropped, took it and broke up the middle, splitting our defense. They tagged along uselessly behind him, not able to catch up. I watched the puck, crouching, ready. He swung his stick and shot, a slap shot coming straight and hard.

I watched it, moved a bit, tried not to think or duck and reached out and picked it off. Easily, perfectly. A save that Ken Dryden would have been proud of.

I was still holding the puck, trying not to let my grin show through my face mask, when I heard it. First there was the applause, just as there always is for a good save, and a smattering of cheers—"Well done! Way to go, goalie!"

And then, over and above the other cheering, I heard a single voice, strong and proud. "Shabash, Rana!" it called. "Shabash, shabash!"

Not believing what I'd heard, I scanned the bleachers. It wasn't too hard to see where the words had come from. Sitting well away from the other parents, his white turban showing clearly in the dim light, was my father. Babli was beside him, clapping furiously, jumping up and down on her seat so hard that her braids were flying out from under her head scarf. "Shabash Rana!" she yelled, waving at me.

After that save and the face-off, our team took the puck and all the action moved to the Safeway goal, which was a good thing. For some reason I was having trouble seeing. I lifted my mask and rubbed at my eyes with my sleeve, looked once more to make sure that Dad and Babli really were there, and then went back to playing hockey.

12

For the next few weeks things went so well that I almost forgot that there had ever been any problems. We kept on winning games and my skating was improving a lot. It looked as though our team was going to finish near the top of our division. I hadn't heard any Hindu comments lately and Les' father made a point of saying hello whenever he saw me.

My father and Babli came to most of the games. Mom wouldn't come, even though we had all asked her to. If it were a Sunday morning game, no one from my family would be there because they'd be at the Sikh temple. That's where I'd be too, if I didn't have a game.

Mom and Dad were understanding about all the Sunday games, even though I knew that some of their friends didn't think much of me playing hockey instead of coming to the temple. And on those Sundays I found that I missed going. It wasn't just hanging around with the other kids after the service; it was more than that. Every Sikh in Dinway showed up at the temple on Sunday mornings, and I missed being part of that. I'd never really thought about it until I began playing hockey, but the temple was important in my life. Just as important as hockey, but in a different way.

I'm not sure how it happened, but one game I noticed that it wasn't just Babli and my dad calling "shabash" when I made a good save. The other parents had picked it up. I'd hear my father first, his voice coming from a different part of the arena than most of the cheering, but then other voices would repeat it. "Shabash, Ron, shabash!" It made me feel good to hear it.

When things go too well in your life you should get suspicious that something nasty is just around the corner. But I wasn't suspicious; I was too busy having a good time.

It happened at our first out-of-town tournament. It wasn't an official tournament, just a few of Dinway's Pee Wee teams traveling to another small town, Malden, to play against their teams. There was no trophy for the team that won; it wasn't really a big deal. But I had never played in another town before and I was looking forward to it.

We left Saturday, about noon. It wasn't a long drive, only about 100 miles, but the school bus the league had borrowed had a flat tire. We were late getting to Malden and everyone was waiting for us, waiting to start the game. Our team was the first to play and Coach Bryson rushed us into the dressing room without even giving us time to think.

We lost, three to two, which meant that we'd have to play the next game at five, just over an hour and a half away. Even while we were changing out of our gear there were Malden parents hanging around, hurrying us up so they could take us to their homes for dinner and then have us back at the arena in time for our next game. All of us from Dinway were to be billeted out that night, because the tournament went on until Sunday afternoon.

There was no one in the dressing room calling my

name, so I picked up my equipment bag and went back into the arena. Coach Bryson was there, talking to a few parents and kids, reading names off a list. I went and stood with the others, waiting to find out who my billet was.

"Ron," the coach read. "You're with Mrs. Cramer. Is Mrs. Cramer here?"

"Yes," said a woman, stepping forward. She was one of the smallest people I had ever seen. She had a tiny head that perched on a long, skinny neck, and her nose was enormous. She had on a bright pink ski jacket and pink slacks and she reminded me of one of those pink birds people put on their lawns. If she'd just lift one foot and tuck it behind the other one, she could stand in for a plastic flamingo any day.

"Who's my billet?" she said, looking around.

"Ron Bains," said the coach and I stepped forward.

"Oh," she said.

"Ron, this is Mrs. Cramer. She and her son Albert will look after you."

I guess Mrs. Cramer hadn't seen me except in goal, in my face mask and helmet. She stared at me, taking in my dark skin, my ghuta.

"Oh," she said again. "But...but I'm awfully sorry. I didn't come here to pick up anyone. You must have misunderstood me. I only wanted to tell you that I...that I've got unexpected company for the weekend and won't be able to take a billet after all."

"Really?" asked the coach. "It would have been considerate of you let the organizers know, so they could have assigned Ron another place to stay. It's a bit late to change your mind; I don't even know who to contact about getting another place for him. Are you sure you don't have room for him? It's just for one night."

"Oh, no," she said. "Couldn't possibly. Sorry. He'll have to stay somewhere else." She turned around and walked away, shaking herself a bit the way a bird does when it's wet. Or when it's got something dirty on its feathers.

I didn't believe that she had other company. I could tell the coach didn't believe her, either. I stared at her pink back as she walked away and wondered why I hadn't thought about the billeting before I agreed to come to Malden, thought about how it could be a problem. Perhaps because things had been going so well I had forgotten about people like Mrs. Cramer. Dinosaur people.

I shouted something in Punjabi at the pink jacket, but she was too far away to hear me. Probably just as well. I'd bet anything she didn't speak Punjabi, but I knew I sounded angry. I *was* angry, I realized. Furious.

The coach didn't speak Punjabi either, but he knew that I was upset.

"Take it easy, Ron," he said, putting an arm around my shoulders. "Don't let it get to you. Maybe she really does have company."

"I won't let her get to me," I said. "Or I'll try not to. But I should have thought about the billeting. I should have known I wouldn't be welcome and I should have stayed home."

"No, you shouldn't have," said the coach. "You're our goalie; we couldn't play in this tournament without you. You have every right to travel with your team and every right to be treated the same way as the others."

"Tell that to Mrs. Cramer's company," I said. "If you can find them. Tell that to her, not that she'll listen."

"Try not to be angry, Ron. I should have remembered how bad it can be sometimes and paid more attention to the billeting arrangements. I know there are many parents here who would have welcomed you into their homes. Don't get upset because of one woman's prejudice."

"I'm not upset," I lied. "Not at all. But I think it would be better if I just went on home, coach. If you can take me to the bus and lend me the money, I'll pay you back. I want to go home."

I did too. Very badly, but I wondered about how pleased my dad would be to see me. Would he think I had let my team down? Had run away rather than staying and fighting?

"You can't go home, Ron. We need you here. We'll figure something out, find you another billet."

"Who?" I asked, looking around. The coach and I were the only people in the arena; all the other players had been picked up by their billets and left. "Maybe Mrs. Cramer has a brother I can stay with. Just get me to the bus station, Coach. I want to go home. And don't start with the 'quitter' stuff. Sir."

"Don't you start with the 'sir' stuff again, Ron. Don't get mad at me and don't let your temper win out. No matter how angry you feel, you've got a responsibility to the rest of your team. And to me."

"Responsibility is going to make a pretty cold bed if I have to sleep on the ice tonight," I said. "You suppose someone will lend me a blanket? It's better if I leave."

"No, it's not. We'll get you a room at the motel where the other coach and I are staying. The hockey league can pay the bill."

"Motel?" I said, wondering what my parents would think when they heard about that. But it might be okay. I'd never stayed in a motel before, but they had TVs, didn't they? And pop machines? I could stay up and watch the late movie if I wanted to, something my parents never let me do.

The coach looked as if he were all set to go into his sportsmanship lecture and I'd heard it before. Did I really want to go home? I decided I didn't. I wanted to stay and play the rest of the tournament. Play it and win it and hope Mrs. Cramer watched every single game.

"You can skip the rest of the lecture, Coach," I said. "I'll stay. I won't let her beat me. The team needs me, right?"

Mr. Bryson smiled at me. "Good for you, Ron. Shabush!"

He didn't pronounce it properly, but I knew what he was trying to say. "Thanks coach," I said. "Let's go."

13

The motel wasn't far from the arena, so the coach and I walked over to it. The man in the office was tall and skinny and wore a big cowboy hat, cowboy boots and a string tie. When he spoke he sounded as if he had been practising for a part in a Western movie. "Howdy, folks," he greeted us. "Part of the hockey gang, right? Figured you were. I've got some rooms booked for you all."

"We're going to need another room," said Mr. Bryson. "For Ron."

"Will it have a TV?" I asked.

"Sure, all the rooms have TV, son. You're too young to be a coach, so I guess you must be one of Dinway's players. What position?"

"Ron's our goalie," said the coach. "We've just had our first game."

"Lost it," I said. "Three to two."

"Yup, I know that," he said. "You played against my son Mike's team. He said it was a tough fight."

He looked at me and grinned. "Matter of fact, Mike was

kind of upset after the game. Last year when he played Dinway there was some kid in goal for one of the teams and he scored five times off him in one game. Mike's been talking for weeks about how he was going to go for ten goals in one game this year, but he came home in a fine state. Seems your new goalie blocked every single one of his shots."

"Oh, " I said. Mike must have been the wing who had made all those dumb shots at the net. He had kept trying to shoot, even when he was too far out to score.

"Guess you were that goalie, right?"

I could feel my cheeks getting hot. "Guess so," I said.

The motel manager laughed. "Good for you, Ron. Mike's got to learn not to count his goals before they're scored. It will do him good to be taken down a peg or two."

"Dad!"

The door behind the office counter had opened and through it I could see what looked like a regular living room, not a motel room. *Probably the motel manager and his son lived back there,* I thought. A kid about my age stood in the doorway, looking mad. It was Mike, the wing who hadn't managed to score; I recognized him from the game.

"Come on, Dad, give me a break! You don't have to tell everyone everything I say!"

"Settle down, son. Didn't mean any harm by it. I was just making conversation with these folks. Didn't know you were listening. Did you hear that this young fellow is the goalie who gave you such a rough time?"

Mike turned and looked at me. "No," he said. "I didn't hear you say that. Was it really you?"

"Yes," I said. "Sorry."

"Hey, we don't have any East Indians on our team. I didn't know you guys played hockey."

"We do now," I said.

"You're good in goal, you know that? Dad was right; I was ticked off when the fat guy wasn't in the net, but it made a better game. And he's pretty good at defense. We only beat you by one."

The motel manager had passed the coach some papers to sign and then he put two keys on the counter. "Rooms 24 and 20," he said. "I guess the other coaches will check in later."

"How come you're staying here?" Mike asked me. "I thought all the players had billets?"

"I thought so, too," said the coach. "But there was a problem with the arrangements for Ron."

The motel manager grinned at us. "You don't say. Let me guess now. The person who was supposed to look after Ron wouldn't by any chance be Mrs. Cramer, would it?"

The coach and I were both surprised. "How did you know that?" asked Mr. Bryson.

"Easy guess," said the manager and laughed. "We know Mrs. Cramer."

"And her son Albert," said Mike. "Boy, is he weird. You're lucky you're not staying with him."

"You know, I reckon whoever set up the billets didn't know about Ron here being different from your usual players from Dinway or they would have given him to someone else, anyone else except Mrs. Cramer. She's mighty particular about who she invites to her house and I don't see Ron being made too welcome."

"And Albert, her kid, he's not allowed to talk to half of the guys on the team," said Mike. "I don't know why he bothers playing hockey."

"Mrs. Cramer won't even buy a Japanese car or eat Chinese food," said the manager, laughing. "She won't speak to me because I'm from Texas and she doesn't like Americans much."

"She doesn't like anyone much," said Mike.

"I sure hope you and Ron don't think all of us here in Malden are like her," the manager said.

"Not any more," said the coach. "Not since we met you two. Come on Ron, let's drop our stuff in the rooms and go grab something to eat."

"Wait a minute," said the manager. "Mike and I have to eat too. It's just the two of us here; my wife died three years ago and we never did learn to cook much except Kraft dinner. We eat out a lot. We'll take you to our favourite restaurant, treat you to some fine dining."

"He means McDonald's," said Mike.

"Thank you," said Mr. Bryson. "We'd enjoy that."

"And," said the manager, "if Ron doesn't mind our bachelor housekeeping, we'd like him to be our billet for the night. Okay, Mike?"

"Sure," said Mike. "You play Burgertime, Ron?"

"A little," I said.

"We'll have a game if you like. I'm good at it."

"I'm not bad myself," I said.

"And you get the top bunk, okay?"

"We didn't offer to take a billet," said the motel manager. "Because there's just the two of us and we have the motel to run, things can get pretty unorganized around here and I didn't think we'd be very good hosts. I figured we'd give the coaches a break on their rooms, a hockey discount, and that would be our contribution to this tournament. But there's no point in your league paying for a room for Ron when Mike's got the bunk beds."

"And the video games," said Mike.

"We're right honoured to have you stay with us, Ron. Now, let's go eat. I'm hungry enough to eat half a dozen of those big McWhatevers."

He hung a "Back in an Hour" sign on the door and we all left.

The coach grinned as he said, "Mike, I think perhaps I should warn you about Ron and those video games. You might not find it so easy to beat him, you know. I've heard he's pretty good, so don't bet your life savings, okay?"

We climbed into a rusty station wagon which coughed and sputtered before it started and headed down the highway towards the golden arches and a couple of McWhatevers.

We had to go back to the arena after dinner and it was late by the time the games finished. But even so, Mike and I stayed up and played Burgertime. I beat him, then he beat me, then he made popcorn and his dad shouted at us to get to bed otherwise we'd be as useless as two greenhorns at a cattle drive when we hit the ice in the morning. It wasn't until I was almost asleep in the top bunk that I realized that this was the first time I'd ever slept over at a white person's house. It didn't feel the way I'd thought it would; I guess I'd been enjoying myself too much to worry about it. As my eyes closed, I found myself wondering why I hadn't been able to go to Les' house when he asked me on Boxing Day. When we got home, after this tournament, I would go. If he asked me again.

In spite of our bad start, our team won the tournament. Just before the buzzer went on the last game, I saw Mrs. Cramer again. She had her big nose pressed right up against the glass behind my net and she was staring at me.

I smiled and waved at her and she turned away. She didn't look very happy, but I felt great!

14

One morning in March as I was walking to the arena for an early practice, I realized that it would be the last practice. Jamboree Week began next Monday, not just in Dinway but right across Canada. The teams played every other team in their division, one team won the trophy for each division, then hockey was over for the year. The arena was already advertising roller skating, which would begin as soon as Jamboree Week was over and they took out the ice.

It didn't seem possible that the months had gone by so quickly. I swung my equipment bag as I walked, thinking about the first practice, when I'd shown up with nothing but my skates and a hockey stick which was too long for me. I'd learned a lot in six months; about hockey and about people. Next year when I went to sign up in September, there wouldn't be any question of letting me join.

I thought a bit about Mom's bridge too, the bridge I had built with my hockey between my world and the rest of Canada. It was there, not too strong yet, but I could cross over now when I wanted to without being afraid. Perhaps it was a dumb idea, that bridge, but I liked it. It helped. Maybe next year....

Next year was too far in the future. I gave up thinking about that and began to concentrate on Jamboree Week. Something told me that our team was going to win the Pee Wee trophy, even if we ended up playing in the finals against that strong Safeway team. We *had* to win. We'd all worked hard. Les had even lost weight, struggling with his diet for months, and he had become a good defense, scoring pretty often. The others had worked too and now we were a *team*, a good team. We deserved to win that trophy. I started whistling as I walked, feeling good, feeling confident.

The good feeling didn't last through the practice. Everyone was quiet and kind of down. I think it was because it was the last practice. Maybe we were already feeling lonely, missing everyone on the team, even though hockey wouldn't be over for another week. Coach Bryson gave a pep talk at the end of the practice and we cheered up some. He'd been a great coach and I hoped I'd get him again next year.

Jamboree Week didn't start off very well. We lost the first game, to a team we'd beaten almost every other time we'd played them. That meant we couldn't lose any more games, or we were out of the play-offs. The Jamboree games tournament is run on a double knock-out system—two losses and too bad!

But after that first game we pulled ourselves together, and began winning. Sometimes not by very much but we stayed in the tournament. On Saturday we won again, which meant that we had only one more game, the game for the trophy, the next day. We'd made it to the finals!

I was nervous about that game. We'd be playing the Safeway team, as I figured, and they were on a winning streak. They'd always been a strong team and the Jamboree results posted in the arena showed that they'd beaten everyone else in the Pee Wee division.

I'd watched a couple of their games and their centre, the one who thought he was Wayne Gretzky, was really moving. He kept scoring and scoring and Safeway kept winning, usually by a big margin. But a little voice inside me told me not to worry. We'd beaten Safeway before and we could beat them again. We were going to win that trophy, I knew it, and I was going to be one of the reasons we won.

I crawled into bed early the night before the final game, and dreamed of large, soft hockey pucks that floated slowly towards me as I stood in the net. I picked them off easily and flung them back on the ice where the other players grabbed them and ate them. "Great roti, Ron," they shouted. "Throw us some more."

Somewhere in my dreams, as I was tossing the pucks that turned into roti, a phone started to ring. I told myself not to worry, that Coach Bryson would answer it, that I musn't leave the net, and kept making slow, graceful saves.

Then I heard footsteps and my father's voice. The dream was gone. My bedside clock said three-thirty when I sat up, realizing that it had been our phone ringing and my father who had answered it. I wondered what was wrong, what had happened that was serious enough for someone to call us at this time of the night. I was suddenly worried for my grandfather in India.

I scrambled out of bed and went downstairs. My father was on the phone in the kitchen, his face strained. "I'll be right there," he said, then hung up.

"Dad? What is it?" My voice was too loud in the silent house and I lowered it. "What's happened? Is Grandfather...."

"Your grandfather's fine as far as I know," he said. "This is a Canadian emergency. The temple is on fire. I'm going there now to see if I can help save it."

The Sikh temple was new, just finished last year. We had all worked on it, from helping with the framing to putting in the windows and painting, watching proudly as it grew into a place of worship for us. I had spent many hours with the other kids, picking up rocks and raking so that we could plant a lawn. My father had built the front porch and stairs by himself.

Almost every Sikh in Dinway had contributed something towards the building—money, materials, their time. We had all built the temple where we all worshipped. Now it was burning!

My father was hurrying upstairs, back to his bedroom. I followed him.

"I'm going with you," I said. "Maybe I can help."

He didn't say anything, just nodded, and we both went into our rooms to get dressed.

Dinway is too small to have a regular fire department. It has a fire chief, a fire station and one big fire truck, but all the firefighters are volunteers. I had a sudden bitter thought, wondering how many volunteer firemen would get out of their beds on a cold March night just to fight a fire in the Sikh temple. They'd turn out fast enough if one of the goray churches was burning, but I'd bet there would be very few who would bother coming to help us.

I was wrong. There must have been twenty firemen in the temple yard. And crowds of people, East Indian and white, watching. Just watching, because even I could see that there was not much anyone could do. I had seen the flames from blocks away and the few jets of water from the firemen's hoses didn't seem to be doing any good at all.

Dad and I got there in time to see the roof fall in with a large shower of sparks. There was a gasp from the crowd and then I heard one firefighter say, "That's it. Can't do anything now. Might as well let her burn out."

My father and I joined a group of men and stood

watching. I had never seen a large fire before, but I could tell that nothing in the building could be saved. The firefighters had done their best, but no one could get anywhere near the temple. The heat from the flames could be felt as far away as where we stood.

I listened to what people were saying and something inside me went hard and cold. It was just like the feeling I get before a hockey game, only worse.

"Arson!" I heard people saying. The fire hadn't been an accident; it had been set deliberately.

I listened harder. It had been two white men who had started it. Two white men with lots of gasoline. The police had already caught them. After lighting the fire, the arsonists had gone to a party and boasted about what they had done. Someone at the party had called both the fire department and the police and the two men had been picked up. The tins that had held the gasoline were still in their truck.

"Why?" I wondered aloud and someone answered me. There had been lay-offs at the mill again. The two arsonists had lost their jobs. They were angry because some of the East Indian workers had kept theirs. And they were drunk.

Anger. Hate. Prejudice. Ugly things. It would take a bigger bridge than the one I had been trying to build to cross over against those emotions.

I was angry, very angry. Angry at the gorays, the smug white ones who hated me and my people because we were different. The gorays who wouldn't take the time to get to know us, to try to understand us, to be our friends.

The dinosaur people. They couldn't even leave our temple alone, but had to destroy it the same way they tried to destroy our confidence, our pride, with their vicious words and their prejudice.

A bridge to the white world? Who needed it? I didn't, not anymore. I'd tried, tried hard, but it wasn't worth it

They hadn't wanted to let me play hockey, had called me names, had refused to billet me in their homes, but I'd kept on trying. Now I wasn't going to try anymore. The gorays weren't the only ones who could hate.

More and more people gathered. The firefighters spent their time controlling the crowd, making sure that everyone stayed safely away from the fire. There was no longer any point in trying to save the temple; there wasn't much left to save. I could see right through it when the wind blew the flames aside, and the porch my father had built was nothing more than a small pile of charred lumber.

I saw Bill Johnson, his big hands looking red and sore as he wound up hoses. What was *he* doing here? I hadn't known he was a volunteer firefighter and hadn't thought he'd ever show up to fight a fire at our temple. But there he was, working, sweating even though it was cold.

And I didn't care. He'd done enough to me. It was too late to try to make it up. He still thought of me as a stinking rag-head and he always would. I didn't care what he thought or did anymore.

The Sikh women were gathered in one corner, away from the fire and I could hear them crying. One voice rose over the rest. "Everything is gone," it said, in Punjabi. "Everything. We don't have the strength to start all over again." The crying grew louder.

Someone touched my arm. It was Les. "Get out of here," I said. "You've got no business here."

"I came with my dad, to see if I could help. Ron, I'm sorry. I know how much the temple means to you."

"My name's not Ron, it's Rana, and I'm East Indian, Sikh, and you're white. Get out of here and leave me alone. Haven't you stinking gorays done enough for one night?"

"Ron...Rana, please." He touched my arm again. I slapped his hand away and turned my back.

"It wasn't me, Rana. It wasn't all of us. Just two dumb drunk guys. You know I don't feel like that about you, about your family. Don't hate me, Ron!"

"Rana," I said. "Ron's gone." I turned back to look at him. His face was shiny in the glow from the flames and something was caught in the corner of his eye. It moved slowly down his cheek, glistening, and he reached up and wiped it away with the sleeve of his jacket.

"Ron is gone," I said again. "And you should be gone, too. Ron's history and so are you. I hate all of you gorays."

"Please, Ron...Rana, I mean. I thought we were friends."

"Well, you thought wrong then. I hate whites. All of them. I hate you, too, you fat slob." I began to walk away, then I stopped and shouted back at him. "And you'd better get your fat ass in goal tomorrow because there's no way I'm playing for a bunch of gorays."

"But...I can't...."

"Play goal, chicken," I said. "Get in that net for the final game. You take the shots for a change, if you're brave enough. I'm sick of hockey. I quit."

I'd tried to leave hockey once before, but Mr. Bryson had talked me out of it. This time no one could change my mind. My bridge had crumbled as the temple burned and I had no way across.

And I didn't want to go across any more.

15

I was still angry the next day. The hard feeling that had settled in my stomach as I watched the temple burn had turned into a ball of ice that wouldn't melt. My father and I had arrived home about six in the morning. He'd slept for a few hours, after Mom made us tea and listened to us talk about what had happened, but I couldn't sleep. I lay on my bed, thinking, feeling the cold lump in my stomach spread and grow until my arms and legs felt cold, too.

The rest of the family left home at noon, to go to a meeting to begin the planning and working that would be needed before we could rebuild the temple.

"I'm sorry we must miss your final game, Rana," my father said. "But this meeting is important. The sooner we can get organized and start thinking about rebuilding, the better everyone will feel. Good luck! I hope you bring home that trophy."

"Sure," I said. "No problem." I didn't bother telling my family that when the game started at two, I wouldn't be on the ice; that I'd given up hockey for good.

About half past one the phone rang. I knew it was Coach Bryson calling, wondering why I wasn't at the arena. I didn't know if Les would tell him what I'd said last night, but it didn't matter. He'd find out, they'd all find out soon enough. When that game started and I wasn't there to handle the net, they'd know that I'd had it with stupid goray games.

I sat in the kitchen, watching the phone while it rang. When it stopped, I took the receiver off the hook, letting it dangle down beside the table. As far as Mr. Bryson, or any white person was concerned, I wasn't home. And if they came looking for me, I wouldn't answer the door.

Then I went upstairs to my room. I took an old turban that my father had given me out of my drawer and sat with it in my hands. Most Sikh boys wear a ghuta until they are in high school, until they feel ready to take on a grown man's turban. There is no ritual for the change-over. It just depends on when you feel that you are mature enough, ready to handle the yards of soft cotton that must be so carefully wrapped. I took off the cloth covering my ghuta.

Slowly, trying to remember all the times I'd watched my father, I wound the turban material around my head. In the bottom drawer was the white cotton shirt my grandfather had sent me from India for my last birthday. It had big, loose sleeves and embroidery all down the open neck. I pulled off my jeans and tee-shirt and put the shirt on, with a pair of white cotton pants that also came from India. I'd never worn either the shirt or the pants before and it felt strange. The shirt draped over the pants and my bare feet looked dark and unfamiliar against the white of the trousers.

When you are baptized into the Sikh religion you are given a knife in a decorated sheath, a "kirpan," which you wear from then on, every day of your life. I didn't have my kirpan yet, but I knew my father had an extra one. I went to his room, found it, slipped my right arm through the strap and settled it on my left hip. There was a full-length mirror in my parents' room and I went over to it. Someone stared back at me from the mirror; a strange, solemn boy, his skin very dark against the white cotton of his shirt, his eyes old and tired. I saw an East Indian man, a proud Sikh in traditional clothes, not a dark Canadian boy trying to hide his race, his religion, behind Canadian clothes and Canadian customs.

The stranger, the serious Sikh man, looked back at me from the mirror.

I should leave Canada, I thought. Yes, I'd go to India, stay with my grandfather. There was no hockey league there, no stupid goray games to waste my time playing. In India, living with my grandfather, I could be me, Rana Bains, and never have to worry about trying to be "Ron" Canadian Ron, rag-head Ron the goalie.

It didn't seem as if I had been standing in front of the mirror for very long, but it must have been longer than I thought because I heard my family moving around in the kitchen. The meeting was over, I realized, as I listened to my parents talking and laughing. *What did they have to laugh about?* I wondered. *What right had they to laugh when the work and the dreams of the whole Sikh community lay under a thick blanket of grey ash?* I straightened my shoulders and went downstairs.

"Rana! What are you doing?" My mother stared at me, trying to hide a smile. "Why the turban, son? Aren't you a bit young for it yet?"

Babli looked at me and giggled. "You look dumb," she said.

But my father wasn't smiling. "The game Rana, your last hockey game. Why aren't you at the arena? Why are you here? How could you forget about the final game?"

"I didn't forget," I said.

"Rana, no!" My father was upset now, his voice rising as he spoke. "You have done so well and we have been so proud of you. How could you let your team down this way?"

"They don't need me. There's no place for me on that team full of stinking gorays."

"No, Rana, no. You are wrong about this. Your team needs you, Mr. Bryson is depending on you. The last game, Rana. How could you not go?"

"They don't need me, Dad. And I don't need them. I've quit hockey forever and I want to go to India and live with Grandfather. I hate hockey; I hate Canada."

"Oh, Rana, you look so silly!" Babli had been trying to keep quiet, but she burst out laughing as she ran past me up the stairs. "Put your other clothes back on," she said.

"Babli!" My mother followed her up the stairs. "Rana does not look silly. He just looks...older."

My father checked his watch. "The game will be nearly finished. Will you come with me to the arena? Perhaps we will be in time to watch the last few minutes; to show your team that you still care if they win or lose."

"I don't care," I said. "Not any more. Not after what they did to the temple."

"Oh. I understand now." He looked at me, concerned. "Rana, you must learn to forget these things, not to let them upset you. You must learn to go on with life."

"Forget?" I almost shouted. "Some stupid drunk gorays burn the temple to the ground and I'm supposed to *forget it* and go on as if nothing has happened?"

"That's what they were, Rana. Two stupid, drunk men. Whether they were white or not doesn't matter. There are ignorant, prejudiced East Indians, too. And many people from the white community were at the meeting today. They want to help us to rebuild the temple. Already they have donated lumber and other material. Many who came were ashamed and upset."

"I don't care," I said, turning around and heading for the stairs. "I don't care that some of them are upset. I don't care what any white person thinks or does any more."

I went slowly up the stairs to my room, very slowly because my turban was slipping down over my eyes and I couldn't see where I was going. I slammed my bedroom door and sat down on the bed.

My father's voice echoed behind me. "Rana, Rana. You are a Canadian. You belong here, not in India. This is your country and hockey is your game. Don't turn your back, Rana. Don't turn your back!"

16

I sat on my bed for a while, trying not to think. Then I got up and re-did my turban. When I looked in the mirror again I didn't seem to look as old as I had earlier. As a matter of fact, Babli was right. I did look silly, the way she looks when she puts on mom's high heels but can't walk in them properly. Maybe I'd forget about the turban for a few years.

I was just about to take it off and fix my ghuta again, when the doorbell rang. I heard my father answer it, then he called to me. "Rana, Les is here."

"I don't want to see him," I called back.

"Rana! You will see your friend. You have things to say to him about the hockey game. Come down at once!" When my father uses that tone of voice, there's no point in arguing with him. He's angry. I took one last look at myself in the mirror, then went reluctantly downstairs.

My father stood beside the open door. "Will you come in, Les?" he asked.

"No, thank you, Mr. Bains. The coach is taking us to

McDonald's and he's picking me up. I can watch for him out here."

"Very well. Then I will leave you and Rana to speak alone." My father went up the stairs into the living room. Les and I stared at each other.

"You look different," he said at last.

"Who cares? What do you want?"

"I just...I just...." He couldn't take his eyes from my turban and I hoped it wasn't slipping again. "We lost, you know," he finally said. "We lost the championship. I played goal, like you said I had to last night. Only I'm not as good as you and I hadn't had any practice in goal this year and that Safeway team was hot. We lost."

The hard, icy lump in my stomach seemed to twist a bit. "I don't care," I said, starting to close the door. But Les reached out and held onto it so it wouldn't shut.

"Listen to me for a minute, Rana. I'm sorry you didn't play today. All the guys were. Coach Bryson said he tried to phone, but no one answered at your house. I had to tell him what happened to the temple and why you were mad and what you said last night. About me being goalie."

"I don't want to talk about it," I said, wishing he'd go away and stop telling me about the game. But he didn't.

"I'm leaving as soon as the coach gets here," he said. "He wants you to come to McDonald's, too."

"No."

"Well, okay. But I just wanted to say...to tell you...I mean, like I had to play goal today, right? And that big centre from the Safeway team, he takes one look at me and shouts, 'Hey, it's the fat guy in goal again. This game's going to be a pushover.'"

"So what? What's that got to do with me?"

"I got mad, Ron. I mean Rana. Real mad. So I fought out there, really fought hard. I was still scared of the puck, scared of being hit, but I was mad and I didn't think about anything but stopping those shots. They only got two goals, you know. I did okay."

"Who cares?" I said. "It's a stupid game and I don't know why anyone cares about it."

"Maybe you should care, Rana. I thought about you during the game today, about how you'd fought all year and you wouldn't give up. I thought about how you'd kept fighting against all the names the guys called you and even when your billet wouldn't take you and when my dad got so mad..."

He stopped and the two of us stood there in silence, me inside the door, Les outside. I wished he'd leave. I didn't want to hear all this talk about hockey. About fighting.

"Have you finished yet?" I asked.

Les sighed. "Okay. I tried. I still want us to be friends, but I guess you don't want to any more."

"No, I don't."

"Because I'm white? Or because I'm fat?"

"Both."

"Good-bye then, Ron. Or Rana. Maybe I'll see you around somewhere."

He turned away from me and walked down the stairs. A car pulled up at the curb and someone honked. Mr. Bryson. I closed the door quickly, before he could see me. "Who cares?" I said again, but my voice sounded thin.

"Rana!" My father came down the stairs. "I was listening to you, Rana. I am ashamed. Les is your friend, but you spoke to him as if he were dirt."

"He's not my friend any more," I said, but it hurt my throat to say the words. "He's not my friend."

"Come, Rana. Put on your shoes and come with me." My father had pulled on his boots and coat and he picked up my runners from the closet floor and handed them to me.

"I don't want to go anywhere, Dad."

"It does not matter what you want, Rana. You will get in the car and come with me. Now." He put one hand on my shoulder and almost pushed me out the door and down the front steps before I even had time to tie the laces on my shoes.

I didn't want to go anywhere, but I didn't have a choice. Dad was angry, angrier than I had ever seen him.

Straightening my turban, I opened the car door and got in. Dad started the engine and backed down the driveway.

I didn't know where we were going, or why. But I knew I didn't want to be in the car with my father. I wanted to be in my bedroom with the door shut so no one could hear me.

My throat hurt and I wanted to cry.

17

My father didn't say anything as he drove. I sat silently for a few blocks, but then I had to ask. "Dad? Please tell me where we're going."

He didn't answer me. "I am ashamed," he had said. Was he so ashamed and angry that he was going to send me away? I'd said that I wanted to go to India and live with my grandfather, but it didn't seem such a good idea any more. I had a horrible thought that my dad was taking me to the airport to put me on a plane. Right now. If he sent me to India, I wouldn't have to worry about hockey any more.

I also wouldn't have to worry about being with Mom and Babli. Or about my paper route, or my school, or my friends from the temple—all of these things suddenly seemed very important to me. I didn't want to go away. I wanted to stay here; in my house, in my town. In my country. Canada.

"Dad?" I said, but my voice was so weak that he didn't hear me. "Dad," I said again. "I didn't really mean it.

About going to India. Please don't make me go. I want to stay."

"No one will send you away, Rana. Now be quiet and look." He had stopped the car in front of the arena. The parking lot was empty, the big doors were wide open and I could see that the ice was already looking wet as it began to melt. A big banner hung over the front door; "Grand Opening of the Roller Skating Season Next Week."

"Do you see, Rana?"

"See what?"

"It is a building, that's all. With no people inside, it has no life. It is a shell, an empty shell." He started the car again and pulled away from the curb. The arena had looked lonely. It made me feel sad, worse than I already felt. Hockey was over; the arena was empty. *It would fill up with kids and parents and coaches again next year,* I thought. *It wouldn't be empty then. But I wouldn't be part of those who came to the arena.*

My father had stopped the car again and I looked up to see why. We were in front of the Sikh temple; what was left of the temple. Smoke still drifted from the pile of lumber and cement and rafters and broken glass and I could smell charred wood even from the car.

But there were people there, more than a dozen of them. Two Sikh men pushed a wheelbarrow and other men pulled charred pieces of wood from the smoking pile and heaped them onto the wheelbarrows. A load of new lumber had already been delivered and I could see a pick-up truck full of cement bricks being unloaded. By two white men. More than half of the people working to clear the temple site were not East Indian, not Sikh. They were white.

"This building is gone, Rana. But it, too, was only a shell. The people who worship here are what matters. And those who will help us rebuild it. As it is the teams who play hockey in the arena who give it life, so it is the people who bring life to the temple. The buildings are empty shells. And I do not wish to see you destroy your friendships because of a shell."

"But the temple is more than the arena."

"Yes, it was sacred to us. And the new one will be built and it, too, will be holy."

My father started the car again and drove away. "It's not the same, Dad," I said.

"Isn't it?"

I didn't answer him. He turned away from the downtown area of Dinway and began to head up the highway. Towards McDonald's.

"I don't want to go there," I said, realizing where he was taking me.

"You will go there, Rana. You will speak to Mr. Bryson and you will apologize for not being at the game today. Then you will speak to the other players and you will tell them you are sorry."

"Dad, I can't do that. You don't understand."

"I understand that you have done a bad thing, Rana. And I think you understand that, too. Everyone can make a mistake and do the wrong thing, but only a strong person can apologize when they know they have made a mistake."

"I can't, Dad, I can't talk to the coach. Or the others. Please don't make me."

"Rana, today you have put on a man's turban. Now you must also take on a man's responsibilities. I think you know what you have to do."

He pulled into McDonald's parking lot, stopped the car and reached across me to open my door.

"Go on, Rana. Go and speak to your coach."

"Dad, please don't make me do this. I can't."

"You can, Rana. And you will. Now go."

I got out of the car and walked towards the restaurant. Walked slowly, as slowly as I could. McDonald's has a big window right across the front of it and I could see my team in there. Les and Brian and the others. And Mr. Bryson. Someone must have seen me too, because suddenly they all turned and stared at me.

I couldn't do it. I turned my back to the restaurant and began to walk back towards the car.

"Ron! Wait." I didn't have to see him to know who had spoken. It was Mr. Bryson.

I walked faster, away from him. My father saw me and got out of the car. He leaned across his open door and shook his head at me. I stopped.

"Why, Ron, why?" Coach Bryson put his hand on my shoulder and I turned around to face him. "How could you do that to your team? Damn it, how could you do it to me?"

The hard lump in my stomach twisted again and for a moment I wondered if I were going to be sick. I didn't answer Mr. Bryson. I didn't know what to say.

"I'm very upset, Ron. No, damn it, I'm angry. Very angry. Never mind being disappointed in you, I'm angry. We were all counting on you and you let us down. You didn't even have the courtesy or the good sportsmanship to phone me and explain. You just didn't show up."

I felt the coldness rise from my stomach to my throat. "I'm sorry, coach," I said.

"Sorry isn't enough. Those boys had a good chance of winning that trophy, but they couldn't do it without you and you knew that. They haven't been that close in a long time. They could have won if you'd been there to help them."

"I said I was sorry," I said. "And my name's not Ron, it's Rana."

"I see. Well I can tell you one thing. Rana has no team spirit, no loyalty to his team. Ron had both those things. Rana may be a good goalie, but he can stay away from any team I coach next year if this is the way he thinks he can treat people who've had faith in him, who've supported him, who have fought for him."

Again I didn't answer him. What could I say?

He sighed and shook his head. "A coach should be above that type of vindictive comment, Ron. Rana. I apologize. I'm disappointed in you, but I'm not angry. Anger and disappointment aren't the same thing and I know that, but sometimes it's hard to tell them apart."

"It's okay, coach. I deserved it. I was wrong."

"Yes Rana, you were. I am an adult and adults are supposed to be able to deal with losing. It shouldn't mean so much to me. But it does. And there are some pretty upset boys in there. You owe them an apology as well. And an explanation."

Through the big window I could see my team. They weren't eating; they were all standing in front of the window, looking at me. No one smiled. They stared and although I hoped they were looking at my turban, I had the feeling that they had barely noticed it; that they were staring at their team-mate, their goalie who hadn't shown up for the championship game. Who had let them down.

"I'll try..." I swallowed. "...try to talk to them. I don't want to."

Mr. Bryson smiled at me, but it wasn't one of his tight, nervous smiles; it was a real one. "Good. You need to do that, Ron. Come on."

"In a minute," I said. "Coach? I think Rana will learn to be a good goalie. And a good team player. If you'll give him a chance."

"Ask me next year, okay? Right now I'm not sure about that. But I'll pick you up a hamburger and fries. A chocolate shake, right? If Rana likes chocolate as much as Ron did." He went back into the restaurant and I was alone in the parking lot once again. My dad called to me. "Go inside, Rana. Go speak to your team. You must."

I looked back at him and when I turned around to face

the restaurant again, Les was there, holding his package of french fries.

"Hi," he said. "The coach said you were coming in. He's getting you a burger."

"I can't," I said.

"You can, you know," said Les. "You've done harder things."

"I don't think I have," I said. "It's pretty hard to admit you've been stupid."

"That's okay," said Les. "Everyone does dumb things sometimes. The guys aren't really mad. I told them about the temple burning down and all of that. They want to know if you're going to play again next year."

"Yes, I am," I said, and suddenly the cold lump which had been in my stomach since last night began to go soft, to melt.

"Let's go inside then," Les said. "Hey, you want one of my fries?"

He held out the bag to me. It was just a bag of McDonald's fries, half of them gone and the rest splattered with catsup, but I looked at them really hard. Then I looked at Les' hand reaching out towards me. After a minute I took a deep breath, straightened my turban again and followed Les into the restaurant.

Faintly behind me I heard my father's voice. "Shabash, Rana." he said. "Shabash!"

About the Author

Ann Walsh is a successful short-story writer, novelist and poet. Ann has written three other novels for young adults: *Moses, Me and Murder, Your Time My Time,* and *The Ghost of Soda Creek.* She has also written a collection of poetry for children, *Across the Stillness.* She has taught in the public school system and also at community colleges. She has lived in various cities in the United States and South Africa, and now lives in Williams Lake, B.C. Ann gives workshops and readings, for young people and adults, across B.C.